Anne Du Lac and the King's Birthright

Anne Du Lac and the King's Birthright

Lon Torman and Rebecca Carroll

CARILLON PUBLISHING

This book is a work of fiction. Names, characters and events are the product of the authors' imagination or are used fictitiously. Any resemblance to actual events, locales, or persons living or dead, is coincidental.

Edited by Erin Willard
Cover design by Roy Migabon
Map design by Rebecca Carroll

Find our more about the authors and upcoming Anne du Lac books at **www.AnneDuLac.com**

ISBN-13: 9780997619508
ISBN-10: 0997619503

Coming in 2017:
Anne du Lac and the Lady's Legacy

Lon Torman dedicates this book to his wife, Carmen.

Rebecca Carroll dedicates this book to her husband John, and to her children Isabel and Jack.

The authors would like to thank the editor of this novel, Erin Willard, for breathing freshness into the story of Anne and Edmond. We also would like to express our great appreciation to Carmen Torman, Raphaela Harkness, Rachel Hernandez, Marcel Gullo de Oliveira, and Rob Kampen for reading the manuscript and offering excellent suggestions.

Prologue

February 542 AD
On the Downs Near Salisbury, England
Early Evening

He had never experienced a wind as biting as this. The solitary man hunched forward as he walked, to better protect his face against the flurries of snow. He bore his heavy armor easily thanks to his own height and extraordinary strength, imperative for all knights; the broadsword at his side alone weighed well over thirty pounds.

My lord will be most unhappy with this news, but who better to tell him than one he trusts?

There were two sentries at the entry to the king's field tent, and both came to attention as the knight appeared out of the darkness. Fisted hands punched armor breast-plates, saluting as the man was recognized and allowed to pass.

Entering, the knight immediately felt the warmth radiating from a makeshift hearth of heated stones on one side of the large tent. The knight and the king were alone except for a page who would appear every few minutes carrying a metal basket of freshly heated stones from the open fire behind the tent. Large wax candles lit the interior of the tent, along with a smaller candle on the table before which the knight stood patiently at attention.

"Ah, Sir Bedivere," King Arthur mumbled, glancing up from his writing. "I will be only a moment or two completing this."

Bedivere tried not to stare at the enormous man, but the king's presence was just too imposing to ignore.

Arthur's appearance was of a man much younger than his seventy-seven years. On the breast of his cassock was sewn a white shield of cloth with a red dragon painted upon it. In blood, some said. Behind him a green metal shield bearing the same red dragon image had been laid against a tent pole. And there . . . across the table, to the king's right . . . lay the famous broadsword in its girdle.

Excalibur. It somehow signals its powers to anyone close by, as if it were alive. As if it could reach out, on its own, and slice its foes in half. It is like having a third warrior in the room.

"Has the gold been moved from the treasury to the vault?" Arthur wrenched Bedivere's attention back from the broadsword.

"Yes, it has been done, sire." Sir Bedivere was having difficulty broaching the news he needed to report. The king laid his pen down and sprinkled fine sand on the parchment to dry the ink. He finally looked up at Bedivere.

"Good." Arthur punctuated the comment with a deep cough. "And are you certain that only those we trust have knowledge of the location of the treasure?"

"Yes, sire. Of those who carried out the task, only two knights and I remain alive. I carry with me two of the three stone disks that together attest the way to the treasure." He handed the larger stone to the king.

Arthur took it and held it in one hand, feeling its weight. It was about six inches in diameter. The edge measured an inch wide. He ran his other hand over the chiseled surface and etched lines carved by a talented sculptor.

"It is well made. You are to have this stone delivered to Sir Pelinore. That it is held in his family's safekeeping shall be known only to Pelinore and his direct descendants. This stone shall be known as the King's Birthright.

"The smaller stone that you carry is to be conveyed into the hands of the Bishop of Canterbury, who has traveled to Wootton Abbey and is awaiting your visit. Guarding it shall become the brothers' burden, and that is the name the stone shall be known by: the Brothers' Burden.

"It will be done as you command, sire."

"Excellent." Arthur handed the larger stone back to Bedivere and paused to reflect on the circumstances that led him to move the gold and jewels from his treasury to a secret location.

"There is betrayal in the air, Bedivere, and I will have no heir of mine looting the kingdom's wealth after I am gone."

Sir Bedivere decided to brave the question. "But why do you fear betrayal, sire?"

"A dream," the king said, his piercing stare boring into Bedivere. "I've had a dream that was as real as this sword that rests on my table." The king waved his hand toward Excalibur. "I saw Sir Gawain in the dream, as if he had come back from the dead. Gawain warned me that if I fight my son Mordred tomorrow, as I have agreed, both Mordred and I shall die and so shall most of our men. Gawain urged me to make a truce for one month and one day, and to offer Mordred generous terms. This will allow Lancelot time to come and rescue me honorably. And then Gawain vanished."

"And your response, sire?"

"I want you to go to Sir Mordred tonight with your brother and the two bishops who stand at the ready here in the encampment. Offer my son reign over Cornwall and Kent during the remainder of my lifetime and the whole of England after I am dead. If he accepts, I shall meet him and sign this arrangement. I have written the offer on this parchment. Take it to him; he will recognize my writing."

"I shall leave immediately."

"Have you any word from Merlin? It is imperative that I speak with him before I encounter Mordred tomorrow."

Bedivere had known this moment would come. The news was very bad, and he steeled himself for the king's reaction.

"Sire," he began, "moments ago, a messenger brought tidings of the passing of Merlin from this world."

"*Passing*?!" Arthur nearly shouted in his booming voice. "Did you say *passing*? Merlin is *dead*? But that is impossible—Merlin is immortal!"

Stunned, the king began to rise from his stool, then slumped back down in near desolation, his hand covering his forehead. Arthur had never shown even his most trusted knights such a sign of weakness, and Bedivere was unprepared for it.

"Aye, sire." Bedivere lowered his voice. "The seer is dead."

"But *how*?"

"Deception. By the Lady of the Lake."

"Explain this."

"It is said that she cast a spell upon the seer. It appears it was a spell Merlin himself had taught her. Under the spell, she tricked the magician into lying in a stone tomb. Then she closed the lid, suffocating him and sealing his doom."

Arthur turned his gaze to the sword at his right. "And perhaps my own doom, as well."

Three Months Later
Wootton Abbey, Near Wells in Glastonia

The Bishop of Canterbury walked quietly along the stony path that wound to the top of the hill next to the abbey. It was the kind of day that foretold a beautiful summer. The rains of April were behind them, and the flowers and grass were again coming to life. A light breeze was in the air. Distant hedgerows divided the land as far as one could see. The bishop sensed that only a kind God in heaven could provide such glory on earth.

Two months earlier, the cleric had received the body of King Arthur from Queen Morgan le Fay, who had specified exactly the words that would be carved on the headstone.

About halfway to the top of the hill, the holy man paused as he glimpsed the former Sir Bedivere, now a hermit, lying prone on the ground before the grave.

The knight had arrived soon after the body of the fallen king was brought to the abbey for burial. He fulfilled his oath to the king by delivering into the care of the bishop a carved stone disk that would be called the Brothers' Burden. Then, speaking few words, he shed his armor and knightly underclothes, exchanging them for the brown cassock worn by the brethren at the abbey.

Now, the former knight lay motionless before the gravestone in silent prayer.

The bishop reflected on the many famous knights who had perished in the great battle for the throne between King Arthur and Mordred, Arthur's illegitimate son. He considered also the many who were involved on the periphery: Merlin the magician, the Lady of the Lake, the Queen of Wales, and so many others.

And what of Excalibur? It has not been seen since.

Some said it was destroyed in the fight. Others said those who feared its power had locked it away. Still others suggested that it was buried in a secret vault with the wealth of the nation. Some even said that the Lady of the Lake had somehow reclaimed it.

The bishop sighed and turned to the grave. Again, as he did almost every day on his midday walk, he read the Latin inscription:

HIC IACET SEPULTUS INCLYTUS REX
ARTHURIUS IN INSULA AVALLONIA.
Here lies buried the renowned King
Arthur in the Isle of Avalon.

burnham

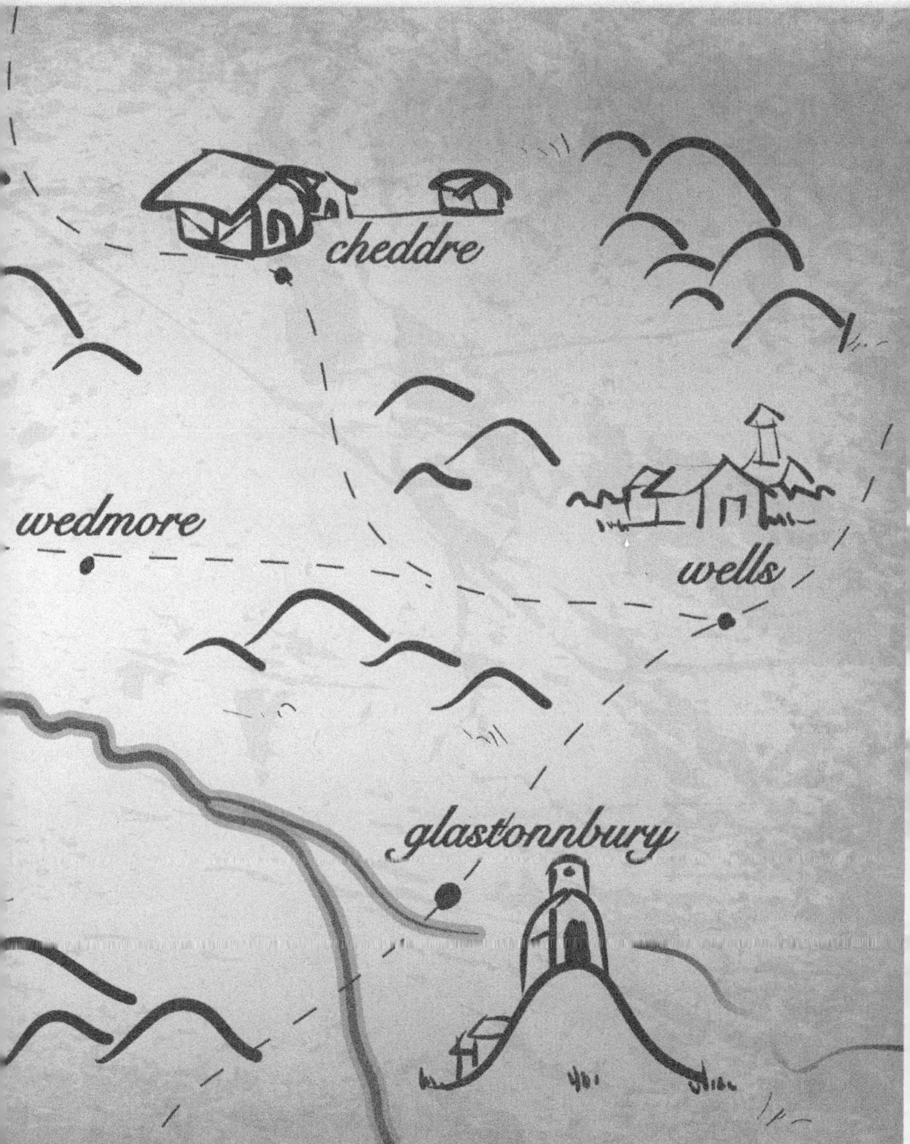
cheddre
wedmore
wells
glastonnbury

CHAPTER 1

Tuesday June 16, 1424 – Late Afternoon
Near the Shore at Burnham-on-Sea

Only a few stray fish in her vicinity underwater could see the dismay draping the face of Anne du Lac as she ascended toward the rowboat above her. She gasped for air as her head broke the surface of the water. Her long tawny hair, tied with a bit of stained twine, wound like a snake behind her as she reached for the edge of the roughly hewn craft, out of breath.

"It's too deep, father," she said to the man sitting alone in the boat.

The man pulled a few strands of his white hair from over one eye. He turned his head toward the bow of the boat. "We haven't the money to buy another net, eh? Come into the boat. There is nothing further to be done here today."

Anne glanced at her father's hands. Ronay du Lac's fingers were deftly knotting small pieces of rope together to form the beginnings of a new net. The sorrow she felt during her dive now turned to anguish as her gaze shifted upward to his eyes, which somehow locked onto hers, as if he could actually see her.

She had been a child when the blindness spread across his vision. If he could see her now, he would know she had evolved into a beautiful fifteen-year-old. Anne knew that didn't matter. Her father would love her no matter how she looked.

"Get in here with me. We'll row for home." He began feeling around for the boat's oars.

Still clutching the side of the boat and treading water, Anne rested her head against the old wood, biting her lip, thinking. After staring briefly at the water, she inhaled with a rasping sound and plunged back into the deep.

Hearing the splash in the water, du Lac smiled and shook his head. He understood his daughter's persistence.

Underwater, Anne followed the boat's anchor rope, her eyes searching for the net. To her right, a large school of fish turned quickly away from her as she descended. Like an underwater wave, the movements of the fish were precisely synchronized. An eel nipped at her from the left.

Down she swam through the cloudy water, her long legs and bare feet kicking strongly behind her.

Then she spotted it, draped over the rocky ocean floor and tracing every crack and crevasse like a death shroud. Her simple pullover dress, bound at her petite waist, billowed like a mushroom cap as she fought her buoyancy and tried to swim deeper. On her face was a look of fierce resolve.

Anne grabbed the net and pulled hard, but instead of yielding to her strength, the net became taut, obviously caught on something. Her lungs were now beginning to scream for air. Anne pulled harder, stretching the net to its limit, when it suddenly recoiled from her hands and floated to an even deeper part of the seabed.

Straining, she tried to lower herself further and was able to bring her fingertips to within inches of the knotted cords before the pain in her lungs forced her to scramble back toward the sunlight above.

Anne broke the water's surface and began to cough, the seawater in her eyes now mixing with tears.

"I can't reach it. I am so sorry, father."

"Come into the boat, Anne. Look here. I'm making a new net. It will be stronger and finer."

Anne climbed into the boat as her father felt about for a wool blanket. He draped it over Anne, who was trying to stifle her sobs.

She fingered the small section of knotted cords that would become a new net. It was only the size of a small purse.

"This will take at least a week or more to finish, Papa."

"It could be worse."

"I don't see how." She grabbed the boat's rudder.

"We could be oyster farmers, you know, and then we wouldn't even need a net," du Lac said.

A smile spread across Anne's face and she chuckled briefly at his words.

"Sometimes, the blind see better, eh?"

"Oh Papa," she sighed. "What are we going to do without a net?"

It was early evening. In their northern latitude, summer's daylight persisted quite late. Anne guided her father as they wearily climbed a gentle hill leading to their cottage.

"What is that?" he asked, pausing to listen to something in the distance. His blindness had caused him to rely more upon his other senses, so they had become heightened well beyond those Anne possessed. "Do you hear that?"

Anne strained to hear the shouting coming from the direction of their cottage. Then she let go of her father's arm and bolted toward the sounds, knowing he could safely navigate the path from memory. "Not again!" She bounded between the rocks along the way. "The bloody fool!"

"Watch your language, Anne," her father admonished.

"Sorry, Papa," she called back as she disappeared over the rise at the top. "I meant to say 'the idiot!' I'll see you at the house—if it's still ours."

Anne rounded the topmost rocks and stopped short to take in the scene before her.

"You really don't have a choice, woman!" Collin Rogers shouted, standing in front of the du Lac cottage. He was addressing Anne's mother, Goody du Lac, who was behind the kitchen window, one shutter closed. Huddled behind her was Anne's younger brother, John, a skinny boy of seven, his hands intertwined in his mother's apron strings.

As she approached a side door, Anne looked back and forth between the burly Collin and the plump Goody.

"Mother?"

"You will not touch him, you mongrel!" Goody barked, her anger still focused on Collin. She punctuated her demand by hurling a small tomato at him. He dodged it with the scowl of a man about to lose his patience—or his nerve.

In his late teens, Collin was tall, muscular, and darkly handsome, and was known to have both the charm and the ethics of a corrupt politician.

"It will be one night's work," Anne heard him say, as he ducked another tomato flying by, which barely missed his head. "And it will save your home!"

"What are you talking about?" Anne stepped closer to Collin.

"You'd better talk some sense into your mother," he replied, without directly answering Anne's question.

"Sense?" Goody du Lac asked. "Does your father know that you petition his tenants, Collin Rogers?"

"My father knows that you can't pay to stay on the land."

"It will be only days before we've enough money from the market. Won't it be, Anne?"

"I'll take my offer and leave you then! You'll be gone soon enough." Collin was now slowly retreating from the flying vegetables.

Anne stopped him with a hand on his arm. Surveying Collin's clothes, she realized that he had failed to dodge several of the edible projectiles, somewhat lessening his charm.

"You said you had an offer?" she asked softly.

"Ah, at least one ear finds my message."

Goody du Lac leaned over the window ledge, waving a large wooden spoon. "I'll not waste any more of our food on you, Collin Rogers, so you'd best be moving along before I use stones." Suddenly, little John ran from the side door and began to collect rocks in a large basket.

"Mother, please stop!" Anne turned to face Collin. "Talk just to me. And quickly."

"This month's rent. Forgotten. Along with the debt your family owes."

"Well, thank you! What did we do to deserve this?"

"No! It is for what you *will* do."

"He wants to take little John, Anne!" shouted Goody du Lac, overhearing part of the conversation between her daughter and Collin. "Who knows what he's involved with? Don't you speak to him!"

"It's *my* family's land, woman!" Collin turned back to Anne and dropped his voice to a near whisper, trying hard to be persuasive. "All I need is help with some of my work."

Anne raised her eyebrows in disbelief. "We all know you don't *work*, Collin. So what do you *really* want?"

"I need your brother to be a lookout. Is that so hard?"

"But he's barely seven, Collin!"

"Have it your way, then." Collin turned as if to leave. "I really don't have time for any more of this."

"It's not right to force anyone into doing something wrong, Collin."

Collin looked back. "It's not something wrong. Look, a nobleman was robbed of his chest of gold and he wants it back. Your brother will simply be helping him."

Anne looked disgusted. "Noblemen make their own justice."

At that moment Anne saw her father arriving, hunched and out of breath.

"What's going on here?" Ronay du Lac asked in an uncharacteristically irritated voice.

Goody du Lac's face brightened as she saw her husband arriving. "It's Rogers's son, husband. He's come to collect our boy instead of the rent."

"What?!"

"He's already leaving, Papa," Anne interjected.

Collin threw up his hands. "Fools! All of—"

Anne grabbed Collin's shirt, pulling him away from her father and drawing his ear close to her mouth. She whispered, "Three hours. By the largest elm tree."

"What?" Collin replied, and then understood. "Ah . . . smart woman!"

Anne continued in a hushed voice, "Now, Collin, you will walk off in a huff or the offer is off."

Collin gritted his teeth. "If this is some sort of trick, Anne, it's you who will be *off*—off our land in less than a fortnight!" He turned, let out an angry expletive for show, and stomped down the path leading away from the house, kicking up dirt with his heels. In a few moments he was out of sight.

Little John put down the basket of stones he had gathered to throw at Collin and ran to his father's side.

Goody du Lac walked briskly from the house to Anne's side, glancing down the pathway that Collin had used to leave them. Once she was sure he had gone, she asked, "What did you tell him?"

"He's gone, Mama," said Anne, without answering her mother's question.

"Good for you!" said her father to Anne. "Shifty fellow, if I ever saw one," he said, pointing to his cloudy eyes.

"Oh, very funny, Ronay," said Goody, aghast at her husband's joke. "Now, inside! All of you!"

She held her husband closely and they entered the house, Anne and little John trailing behind.

"Ah, wife," he said. "Sadly, there was no catch to be had today."

A smile broke across her face. "Good! Then you won't smell of fish tonight, Ronay."

Now he was also smiling. "Aha! A bright side to everything, my love."

CHAPTER 2

ANNE WAS LYING ON HER pallet, doing her best to ward off the fatigue that normally resulted from a day on the open water, filled with swimming combined with the sun and sea air. She waited for Collin's return, regretting her plan to replace John. She was only going to offer herself in order to ensure peace for her parents from Collin's threats.

She sometimes wondered whether her family could ever be free of the limits imposed by their station in life. The boundaries of her life had felt oppressive to her for as long as she could remember. Since the blindness had overcome her father, each day was more or less the same.

Ronay du Lac had a unique sense of humor, where others in his condition would only convey bitterness at the state of their lives. Anne's young brother would not be ready to assist their father for some years yet, and their father could not fish without a set of working eyes at his side. So it was up to her.

Except in the worst weather, Anne and her father were on the water each day, leaving her little time for friendships.

Anne loved her parents, and especially appreciated the way they could provide for the family's needs with so little to draw upon from their meager existence. Most of all she loved her father. As she often did, Anne absently caressed the golden ring on her right finger that he had given to her when she turned thirteen years old. "This belonged to my mother and, before my mother, to her mother," he had said. "It has been passed down through our family for many generations and now I give it to you. Wear it in remembrance of the many who have gone before you. Treasure it, as we treasure you."

From time to time on market days, Anne would join her father in the nearby village. It was the only time that she would see young people of her age. She also saw the wealthy gentry strutting around in their self-importance. She was amazed at the extravagance of their lives.

She had one true friend: Bernadette Baker. As her last name implied, Bernadette's father owned the village bakery, a place of wonderful smells and tastes, a feast for senses that were too often limited to the smell of fish. Bernadette's mother was a seamstress who was often employed by the nearby landed gentry eager to show off new wardrobes with every changing season.

A few days earlier, Bernadette had seen Anne at the market and invited her to her home above the bakery for lunch. There, over a luncheon of tea and delicious cakes, Bernadette and Anne had taken time to dream together. Nearby, Bernadette's mother, whom Anne called "Auntie," had been sewing a gown to be worn at a village ball.

"And who is that for, Auntie?"

"It is for the governor's daughter, who will wear this at the harvest ball in a few months."

"And what is she like?" Anne had continued to prod.

"Ah, Anne. The governor's daughter has always received everything she has asked for, and she is never afraid to ask. Her position in life makes this possible."

Anne's eyes had brightened at this, and she had smiled mischievously. "But Auntie, does *my* position in life permit *me* to ask anything, and have it from you?"

"Anything? Why don't you try me?"

"Here goes: May I have another piece of cake, Auntie?"

Bernadette's mother had chuckled and replied, "Of course you may, *your highness*," and Anne reached for another pastry. Bernadette couldn't keep from laughing, and the other two joined in.

Later that afternoon, Bernadette had accompanied Anne part of the way back to the du Lac cottage, which was about an hour's walk from the village. The dusty path was little more than a trail and meandered beside meadows and ponds and through dense woods. Kicking random rocks ahead of them as they walked, Anne hummed a tune she had heard played by a troubadour in the village.

"You like music, don't you?" Bernadette remarked, her dark brown eyes studying Anne. Berdie's long black hair flowed over her muscular shoulders and arms.

"Yes. I've often thought that if I had a recorder or a flute, I might be able to practice on the water while my father and I are waiting for fish to swim into our net."

"Is that all? Wouldn't you want something more to come from your practice? Wouldn't you want to be in some orchestra that entertains the gentry?"

"No. I would never be accepted," said Anne.

"And why not, I ask you?"

"Because people of our station in life never have a chance to do such special things. You know that."

"But you can wish. You can dream. Can't you, Anne?"

"I suppose so. But what's the point? No, Berdie. Dreaming about a different life is a waste of time. Besides, people of noble birth care little about us. I think I shall never know the type of adventure that comes so easily to them."

The two girls walked on silently. A summer breeze flowing from the west had broken through the heat of the afternoon, making the walk more pleasant by sweeping the road dust away like an invisible broom.

Also riding the breeze was the sound of horses' hooves. The road was generally considered safe for those journeying on foot. But this section of the trail was wedged between the banks of ponds on both their left and right sides and provided almost no space off the path.

"Wait! Be still." Bernadette's index finger touched her lips as she listened intently. "Do you hear that? Riders are coming very fast. Move ahead quickly! We must get away from the narrow banks or we could be struck by the horses!"

Instantly, Anne and Bernadette lifted their dresses from the path so they could run more easily. They sprinted forward as the hoofbeats grew louder behind them. But Anne knew instinctively there wouldn't be enough time to get past the ponds.

In seconds, two riders were right behind them, racing along the narrow straightaway, not even slowing though the riders saw the two girls in the road.

Anne looked back briefly as the front horse closed the gap between them. *The rider sees me. Why doesn't he rein in the horse? Is he trying to kill me?*

She ran out of thinking time. "Jump, Berdie!" she called, and grabbing Bernadette's wrist, yanked her friend off the path. As both fell into the pond, the two horses raced past them.

"Idiots! Fools!" Anne called after the riders as she regained her footing.

Standing up in water up to their thighs, Bernadette studied Anne. Her wet hair fell on all sides, water dripping down her back. Berdie saw tiny red rivulets trickling down Anne's arm. "Your arm's bleeding, Anne. And your dress is soaked."

"Well, so is yours, Berdie." Anne lifted her arm to see what damage there was. "I'm cut," she said in a matter-of-fact way, splashing water on the wound. Probably, she thought, the scratches were the result of scraping her arm along the stony bottom of the pond when she fell into the water.

She brushed off her friend's concern. "Nothing to worry about. I always mend quickly."

The two friends made their way back onto the path. Anne reached down with both hands, and lifting her dress, twisted the fabric tightly in her hands, squeezing out water from the pond. Bernadette did the same.

"Did you get a look at the riders?" Anne asked.

"Yes. A man in uniform followed by a very well-dressed woman in riding boots. I'm sure they saw us being pushed off the track."

Anne wrinkled her nose in contempt. "So there it is. Just as I've said. Nobility cares little for us common folk. The riders didn't even return to find out whether we were hurt."

Both had fallen silent as they began walking again along the path. Anne listened to the noise caused by unseen insects in the trees above them. The high pitched squeal of cicadas grew louder as they approached each infested tree, then softer after they passed it by. As raucous as the noise was, Anne somehow appreciated the monotonous sound, broken from time to time by the croak of a frog or two in nearby ponds. Her dress was drying quickly in the warm breeze of the early summer afternoon.

"I can't get that gown Auntie was sewing out of my mind," said Anne, breaking the silence. "Even though I know I shall never be able to afford something so beautiful."

"I see these noblemen and their wives only from a distance," Bernadette said. "But sometimes I think that's for the best."

"Why?"

"Because I hear my mum and dad talking about the way of life of the nobility, and I often wonder whether I would ever want to be part of their reality. They know no bounds."

"Oh, it can't be that bad," Anne remarked.

Living right in the village, Bernadette's parents heard many stories and frequently talked about what they heard, especially after a few cups of wine, even when their daughter was present.

Bernadette looked at her friend, wondering whether she should tell Anne some of the details she had heard, about what happens after the balls and the parties ended at night. She decided not to.

Now, lying in bed, Anne contemplated her life. Hers was a life of purpose and loving relationships. But it was also a life without excitement. She often wondered what it would be like to be swept up in doing new and interesting things.

Ah, well. Even if I wanted to be, I shall never be in a position to meet those of higher station, or be thrilled by new adventures and events, so why should I even be thinking about it at all?

Anne remembered the good times she had with her father before and after the blindness set in. She always admired his ability to stay the course, no matter the task or hardship at hand. Even when their net was lost in the water that day, her father was immediately ready to fashion a new one without a single complaint.

She was eight years old when her father announced that she was old enough to accompany him in the boat for a day of fishing. It was at dinner one early spring evening.

"Tomorrow, Anne, you will help me cast our net upon the water."

The feeling of excitement was memorable. Goody had protested that her daughter was still too young to leave her mother's side.

"No, my love," Ronay had replied. "She can swim like a fish, and she's more intelligent than most girls of her age. It's time she experienced life in the elements. She's ready."

To Anne, it had seemed like she could climb any hill as long as she had her father's confidence.

And so she would accompany him on the boat frequently, listening to him and learning about nature, life, people, and empires. He taught her simple things, like how to tie rope together to form a net that would test well against the weight of a very large catch of fish. He also taught her how to outwit predators of the deep that might attack a lone swimmer far away from shore. And he used nature's own examples—sharks, eels, pilot fish, and more—to teach her about humankind.

Then one day his eyes began to cloud over, perhaps the result of an illness that no one could explain. Anne felt great personal pain at the onset of her father's blindness, as she took over more and more of his daily duties. One day she asked her father why the story of their lives was punctuated by painful experiences.

She never forgot her father's reply. "Experiences in life, daughter, are just like the fish nets we use on our boat. The water flows through the net, leaving us with the catch. Similarly, each painful experience is like a net. The pain flows away, but leaves us stronger so we can face greater challenges."

Anne could never have imagined at those times that one day she would hold the fate of a nation in her hands.

CHAPTER 3

THE HALF-MOON WAS BEHIND A dense cloud later that night, barely visible. There was no light to be seen in the windows of the du Lac house.

Suddenly, the silence was broken by the grating sound of a door opening. Nearby, Collin waited behind a large elm tree and strained to see movement from the direction of the house. He was wearing dark clothes and a leather skullcap. A shadow crept out a side door.

"Psst . . . Johnny boy," he whispered in the direction of the house, spotting movement and waving in that direction. "Over here," he said in a louder voice.

"Shhh," replied the shadow.

"John du Lac?"

"Shhh," replied the shadow, again. "You'll wake them."

Suddenly Collin recognized the shadow's true identity.

"Oh no! Not you! Go back and fetch your brother, Anne!"

"He's seven years old," said the shadow. "You'll have a far better lookout in me, Collin."

"Forget it!" Collin said. "A woman! I'm not leaving without John, do you understand? You can't replace him, even if you *are* wearing his pants. You *need* me to forgive your debt and rent."

"You need a lookout and you need one now, right?"

Collin bit his lip, thinking.

Anne pressed her argument home. "So how about if you forget that I happen to wear a dress most of the day, and let's get on with it?"

Collin said nothing, thinking. He sighed, resigned now to a change in plans. "Follow me. The horse is this way." He turned away from the house and started walking.

Anne was smiling as they picked their way along the path into the dark woods. When she thought Collin wasn't looking, she adjusted the ill-fitting pants with a wiggle.

"You'll have to act less like a—a—girl," mumbled Collin.

Anne lifted one eyebrow. "Only if you act less like a fool."

CHAPTER 4

Later That Same Tuesday Evening
Highbridge

ANNE FELT COLLIN LEAN BACK into her as he pulled at the horse's reins. Riding behind Collin on a saddle made for one person was no fun, Anne thought. Even getting into the saddle had been a challenge.

Collin was easily up and seated on the horse. He had turned to Anne below and said, "What are you waiting for? Mount up."

Anne looked up at the saddle pommel, then the seat and cantle. Pretty much all the sitting room was taken up by Collin. There didn't seem to be any room left for her. "How do I do this?" she asked him.

Collin's voice was thick with frustration. "First, it's a woman. Then, it's a woman who can't even mount a horse. The prospects for this night are getting dimmer and dimmer."

"What do you mean, dimmer? It's already plenty dark," she retorted sharply. "Now tell me how to do this, will you?"

It had taken three tries, one of which had failed so badly that Anne had fallen to the dirt path, landing on her rear. But she had finally made it into the saddle and reached around Collin's waist to keep from falling off as they rode away from her parents' cottage.

"Where are we going?" she asked the back of his neck.

"To a manor house not far from here. Now hold on." He shook the reins.

Thirty minutes later, Anne was tiptoeing behind Collin as they emerged from dense scrub brush onto a lush lawn that sloped upward. Anne tried to imagine what would happen when they arrived at the manor.

Normally, fog would reach north from Hunspill at this time of year. On this night, however, a light sea breeze from the west kept the fog at bay. The waning half-moon provided a thin wash of light at ground level, illuminating the Highbridge estate.

A formidable ten-foot-high castle-like stone wall encircled the compound, broken only by a heavy wooden gate fronted by a dirt forecourt.

She stopped in her tracks when Collin reached back toward her with one hand; with his other hand he signaled her to be quiet, then pointed toward the gate ahead. Anne squinted into the near-darkness, barely seeing two guards who were lounging against the stone wall, just outside the gate. The pair was an improbable sight. One guard was older, tall, and rail thin. The other was short and rotund. Both were equally inebriated.

Flushed and smiling, the thin guard took a swig from a metal mug and swirled the remains in the bottom of the cup. Both sentries were oblivious to Anne and Collin, who were now just two shadows slinking through the greenery.

Suddenly, Anne heard a loud clacking sound as keys were inserted in the gate lock from the inside. She watched as the guardsmen hastily shot upright, standing at attention.

"Psst—Perkins!" the short guard whispered, pointing to the metal cup still in the thin guard's hand.

"Oh. Right." Perkins hurled the mug into nearby bushes, where it struck a blow to one side of Collin's head.

"Bloody hell—" Collin started to say before Anne threw her hand over his mouth to muffle the cry.

The guards heard nothing except the loud creaking of a small door within the gate. A moment later, a servant in bright red livery emerged through the door holding a wooden bucket.

"At ease, gentlemen." The servant nodded to Perkins. To the short guard, he said, "And how are you this eve, Salgar?"

The two sentries slumped back into their lounging poses.

"Jons, we thought you was the night inspection," Salgar said to the servant, a tone of relief in his voice.

"Yeah," Perkins said, "I just throwed out me last cup o' brew fer nuthin'!"

Nearby, Anne looked at Collin, still rubbing his head where the mug had bruised him. She opened both hands and raised her eyebrows as if to say *shouldn't we get away from here*? He shook his head, signaling patience.

"Maybe you threw your cup away because I have such a *commanding* presence," joked the servant, dropping the bucket to the ground. He withdrew one of the unlit torches that fitted into the wall on the side of the gate and readied the torch for fire.

"How 'bout you *command* me up some more ale, Jons?" Perkins mumbled as he squatted on a short barrel, removed his helmet and prepared to sleep off his mugful.

"Not likely I can help you with that," said Jons.

Anne watched as the servant lit the torches on both sides of the gate and replaced them in their sconces. He returned his tinderbox to the bucket, which he picked up and carried with him as he headed back through the gate, locking it behind him.

Perkins was asleep a moment later. Salgar sat on a wooden crate and removed his helmet for comfort in the warm, humid night. His eyelids almost immediately drooped before they closed in a deep sleep.

Wasting no time, Collin crept silently toward Salgar. His hand held the mug that Perkins had tossed into the bushes minutes ago.

Anne could hardly hear the sound of the mug crashing against Salgar's head. Perkins remained motionless as Salgar collapsed downward, unconscious. Both Anne and Collin reached out and grabbed his arms to control his fall and try to reduce the noise his armor would otherwise make as he slid to the ground.

Collin rushed to the sleeping Perkins's side and, with both hands, raised the heavy mug above the guard's head before striking a silent blow on Perkins's forehead. Again, Collin and Anne held the guard's arms to cushion his fall.

Anne shook Perkins's hand, trying to coax a response, but there was none. "He's out, too" she said.

"Course he is," Collin whispered. "Not a word will be coming from either of their mouths for a fair bit of time, I reckon. Now, let's get these blokes into the bushes."

Collin grasped both of Perkins's wrists and began to drag the unconscious sentry across the forecourt, toward the tree line.

"Collin, I know you aren't leaving me with this fat one to move, right?"

"You want to get it over with or not? Better hurry."

With a look of disgust Anne dragged Salgar's huge mass through the dirt behind Collin and Perkins. She could feel matters going downhill already.

CHAPTER 5

ABOUT TWENTY MINUTES LATER, ANNE and Collin were shadows no longer. They were now dressed in the guardsmen's clothes, minus the armor. Together they had scurried over the top of the outer wall using a large length of rope that Collin had previously hidden behind a tree.

Once inside the compound they ran along the interior side of the elliptical stone wall, slowing down at a point where it neared the two-story manor house.

Collin, now draped in the rope they had used to scale the wall, began to count windows. At his side, Anne sniffed at the sleeve of the sentry uniform she had borrowed from Perkins. *Just wonderful*, she sniffed, wrinkling her nose at the smell of sour ale combined with weeks of sweat. "What's next?"

"Shhh," whispered Collin, holding a finger to his lips.

Without warning, Anne felt herself being shoved against the wall. Collin covered her mouth with his hand, just as another guard rounded a corner of the manor. They both held their breaths. The guard looked up, as if he was checking the weather, then did an about-face and marched back out of sight.

Exhaling, Anne turned her head away from Collin's hand to be able to speak. "I thought there were only two guards!"

"So, maybe I lied a little. Now, come with me and be silent."

He headed for a tree towering over the house. It had a large limb that reached out toward a window on the second floor. She watched as Collin began to climb. Reaching the long branch, he looped the rope over a higher limb and tied one end around his waist. She realized that he was planning to use the lower limb as a bridge to the manor house.

"All right. C'mon up here," Collin said to Anne, standing below.

"Why, exactly?"

"See the window over there? In there is what we're after."

"Why don't I just stay right here to keep watch?"

"No! Get up here or you get nothing, and you and your family can starve for all I care. I'll tell you right now that you don't make for a very good thief."

"I'm not supposed to be a thief! I'm only supposed to be a lookout, remember?"

Anne rubbed her hands together for a few moments, and then began to climb the tree, one branch at a time. When she reached the overhanging branch, Collin removed his leather skullcap and placed it on Anne's head, stuffing her long hair under it.

"Here. Keep this cap on your head. If anything should happen, play it off like you're a boy. Got it?"

"*If anything should happen*?!"

"Oh . . . There's nothing to worry about. This is a small country manor with a guard or three. That's all. And afterward, they'll be looking for two men, not a man and a woman."

As he spoke, Collin tied the loose end of the rope, which was still draped over a higher branch, around her body and under her arms. "This will protect you in case you should fall off the tree."

What happened next occurred before she could react. Without warning, he heaved her off the branch and immediately started to rein in the rope, causing her to swing back and forth from the higher limb over which the rope was draped.

Anne instinctively covered her eyes with both hands as the rope played. Collin, still holding onto his end of the rope, pulled faster, nudging Anne and the rope into small circles between the trunk of the tree and the house, rising to the level with the window.

"You'll need your hands to grab onto the window," he said in a hushed, but intense, voice. "Take them from your eyes."

"No! You didn't talk about swinging into a building."

"Hey look—we had a deal!"

"Get me down! *Pleeeeeeease*!"

"Shhh! I can't believe this! Okay . . . I'm going to bring you back."

Collin began to further pull on the rope swinging her back onto the limb with him. He needed to calm her down. "Look, I'll do it, and you can go back to being the lookout."

Anne was hauled back into the tree. He placed both hands on her shoulders as she faced him, in a feeble attempt to soothe her. At first she didn't move, then she opened her eyes, looking straight at Collin. Calm contempt was now written on her face. "Really? Me? A lookout?!"

"If that's what you want," said Collin with a smug expression. "Now *look out* for the wall." And with a very firm shove, he again sent her swinging toward the house like the pendulum rod of an upside-down metronome.

At the top of the arc, she was still below the window's height. Collin pulled feverishly on the rope, elevating Anne's arc as she flew back toward the tree. She reached out to grab a branch, but missed it and felt herself swinging back toward the manor house.

Now Anne saw a window ahead of her, open to catch whatever breeze the warm night would provide. The opening would be at the top of the rope's swinging arc. She reached her arms out in a feeble attempt to cushion herself against the possibility of hitting the wall.

At just the right moment Collin let the rope go slack, and Anne flew through the open window, hitting the wooden floor inside and rolling to a stop against a very old oak desk. She sat up, rubbed her head, and looked around at what appeared in the moonlight to be an expensively furnished drawing room. Gilt tapestries adorned the walls, and as she stood she saw a finely carved desk with a jar of curing feathers sitting on its surface.

She stood and tiptoed back to the window, leaning out toward the tree where Collin waited.

"You fool!" she hissed furiously, "I can't believe you did that!"

"Hey, we're almost there. Now look for a red box with a snake painted on it. It's locked up somewhere in there."

Shaking her head in disbelief, Anne untied the rope from her waist and retied it to a chair so it wouldn't slide out the window and to the ground below. She then began to look for the box on every table and behind all the drapes and tapestries. Leaning back out the window, she said in a hushed voice, "I don't see it anywhere, Collin."

"It won't be obvious, but it's definitely in that room."

She walked slowly around the drawing room, still not seeing anything remotely resembling a red box. She decided to rest a moment and think about where it could be.

As she sat down on a bench draped in red cloth, she heard the dull clunk of metal and felt something strange against the back of her legs. Startled, she pulled the cloth to one side, revealing the bench was actually a chest. It was held shut by an enormous iron lock.

Glancing again around the room, Anne spotted a pair of crossed axes adorning the far wall. She withdrew one axe and carried it over to the chest. She raised it high as if she was preparing to let it fall against the lock, but was reconsidering, afraid the resulting noise would be too loud.

"Anne!" called Collin in a hushed but urgent tone of voice.

"What, Collin?" She still held the axe high over her head.

"Not with the axe, Anne! Pick the lock. The axe will bring a small army on our heads."

"Small army?! You said there were two or three guards!"

"Yes, but I didn't say these two or three were the *only* guards."

Pinching her lips together in irritation, Anne spun around and returned the axe to its wall hook. She went back to the window. Looking across at Collin in the tree, she whispered: "How do you pick a lock?"

"Look for anything that's long and thin."

Glancing around the room, Anne spotted a stiletto knife on a table. She turned toward Collin and held it up with an inquiring look.

"Yeah. That'll do it. Stick the point in the lock and jiggle it about. You're new to it, so it may take a while."

Though doubtful, she pushed the end of the knife into the lock and wiggled it. To her utter surprise, the lock came open. Anne turned her head to look across at Collin triumphantly. He bowed his head in admiration.

She began to rummage through the large chest, and, under bundles of parchment rolls, located a red box large enough to hold a small melon. There was a gold dragon painted on its red lacquered lid. Remembering Collin's earlier description, she imagined that the box was filled with gold and therefore exerted all of her strength to lift it out of the chest. However, its contents were much lighter than she had anticipated and she pulled upward with far too much force, lost her balance, and stumbled backward.

Groping for some support, her hand clutched a tapestry, causing it to tear from the wall, its brass posts clattering on the wooden floor.

When quiet at last replaced what had seemed like interminable noise, she sat motionless, listening . . . and heard the voices of people stirring within the manor house.

Anne rushed to the window. "Collin! Get me out of here!"

Collin was already nearing the bottom of the tree, half climbing, half jumping.

The voices were getting louder and closer, and torchlight began to stream through the crack under the drawing room door. Anne heard Collin calling from below the window. "Unless you're fond of torture, I suggest you move quickly!"

She fumbled for the end of the rope that had carried her from the tree in the first place, locating it beneath the window where she had tied it to the leg of a chair. Anne undid the knot and retied the rope to the leg of the solid oak desk, the other end still dangling over the windowsill to the outside.

Climbing out the window, the box barely held under one arm, she tried to inch her way down the rope. But her progress was much too slow, hindered by the box.

Her head was scarcely below the level of the window when she heard the door to the drawing room swing open, its latch banging against one wall. Then she heard the sounds of several soldiers in armor storming into the room. "They've taken it!" came a shout.

"Throw the box down," called Collin from below. "Hurry! I'll catch it. And then I'll catch you, as well."

Anne dropped the box. Collin caught it easily.

"Look outside!" She heard one of the soldiers from within the drawing room.

Anne slid down the rope, now level with the top of the first-floor window, her eyes shut, unwilling to look down. She was ready to let go. "OK, Collin, here I come. Please don't drop me."

No response.

"Collin?"

Anne plummeted to the ground, a gathering of bushes breaking her fall. Looking up, she saw two guardsmen pointing down at her through the window above.

"Collin?" she called again, looking around the now-empty expanse between the manor house and the estate's perimeter wall.

He was nowhere in sight.

As she fainted, she caught sight of several sentries in armor, swords drawn, running at her from both sides.

CHAPTER 6

AWAKENING VERY SLOWLY, EYES CLOSED, the first thing Anne sensed were the knotted ropes encircling her hands and legs. Next, she felt the cold slate floor against her cheek as she lay inert, not daring to move. She heard a conversation, but somehow could not bring herself to open her eyes.

"And the other one?" one of the voices asked.

"Made off with it, m'lord. We have parties searching, but there is little in the way of tracks. We need a direction to start with."

Anne half opened one eye, enough to see, but not enough to be seen awake. There were three men in the room, which appeared to be a large banquet hall in the manor house. It was capped by a high ceiling that echoed the conversation below back to the huge table lined with benches and stretching across the center of the space.

Lord Aylesbury, the lord of the manor, looked even older than his eighty-six years. A trimmed gray beard adorned his face. Gray hair fell over his ears from the bald landscape on top of his head. She noticed his royal blue robes were tailored to his exact height. They just touched the floor behind the nobleman's stooped and shaky frame as he paced back and forth behind a large oak chair.

Next to the chair stood a very tall and very dashing military captain, with epaulets on his shoulders that bore the polished metal stripes of his rank and were perched atop a white tunic bearing a blue crest. The mop of black hair on the young captain's head seemed to emphasize his clean-shaven face; his turquoise eyes were visible even in the dim candlelight. His pressed uniform couldn't hide the fact that he was quite muscular, and Anne couldn't help but notice.

Hmmm, she thought. *Quite a handsome one, he is.*

Standing beside her silent body on the floor was the lord's chief bodyguard, a giant man of obvious brute strength. His face was tanned and scarred like someone who had known adventure, yet there was emptiness about him. He could pass for a hero who had not seen enough victories or a villain who had seen more than enough bloodshed.

"She has fainted, Dorsay? Are you sure?" Lord Aylesbury asked the bodyguard, glancing again at the motionless form huddled on the granite floor. "If she doesn't awaken, where will we be then?"

"I can make her come to, m'lord."

"I think not, Dorsay."

Anne's hair had fallen out of her cap and it was quite obvious to the three men that she was not a boy, but a young woman. Suddenly reminded of her situation, she jolted upright, only to be stopped by the series of ropes binding her hands and feet.

"She's awake," said Dorsay, kneeling next to Anne. His huge hand scooped the cloth of her tunic and effortlessly lifted her onto a small stool, almost like a child lifting a toy from the floor. She thought to bolt away, but as she stood, Dorsay grabbed her shoulder and pounded her back down onto the stool.

"Who are you and who sent you?!" shouted the furious Lord Aylesbury. He leaned over and crowded into her face, spittle hitting her forehead as he spoke. She turned her face to one side, away from his rotten breath.

Dorsay tightened his grip on her shoulder enough to make her squirm in pain. "Look at me! Best you talk."

"Indeed," added Aylesbury.

Anne was speechless. A piercing headache made it all the more confusing. "I . . . uhhh . . . what?"

"Who sent you?" repeated Aylesbury.

"No doubt she will try to keep it from us, my lord," Dorsay said.

Anne blinked a few times. "Keep what from you?"

Dorsay tightened his grip still further. Anne cried out in pain.

"You will address Lord Aylesbury as 'my lord' or 'your grace,'" Dorsay said through clenched teeth.

Showing signs of compassion, the handsome captain, who had been standing by silently, suddenly entered the exchange. "Dorsay, she may be a thief and she may eventually be executed, but we should be gentle here."

Dorsay turned to the captain, yielding to rank with an almost sarcastic tone. "Yes . . . Edmond." He relaxed his grip on Anne.

Executed?! Anne was finding it difficult to speak through her dry lips. She had long wondered what it was like to be in the company of those of higher station in life, but she never, ever, envisioned the brutality she had just experienced.

Lord Aylesbury was becoming more and more impatient. "Where is the King's Birthright, the stone disk?"

Anne's eyes widened, perplexed. "Birthright? I know nothing of any stone . . . "

Dorsay's fingers dug into her shoulder again.

" . . . my lord," she added.

"Did you not take a locked box with a dragon upon it?" The captain's voice was gentle, as he motioned to Dorsay to lessen the pressure on her shoulder.

"I do not have it, uh, *my lord*," she replied.

"Then please explain something to me," Aylesbury said, still angry. "Why is it not in my study where I last secured it? Your accomplice has made off with it, no doubt."

Anne groaned. "Collin took it, my lord, and . . ."

"And left you here to rot, I think," Aylesbury said. "Collin who? What is his surname? Where is he from?"

"Collin Rogers. I am his father's tenant."

Captain Edmond stepped in again. "Do you even know what it is that you took?"

"I was told we were returning a small chest of gold stolen from some noble."

Aylesbury was still gruff. "What noble? What is his title?"

Her eyes started to water. "I don't know, your grace."

"You lie!" Dorsay shouted.

She felt her body beginning to tremble and took a deep breath. This had a brief calming effect. Anne looked at each one in turn before speaking. "I was never given the noble's name, truly! Only when I lifted the box did I think it too light for the gold that was supposed to be within. By then, it was too late."

Lord Aylesbury had had enough. He turned in a fury and began to storm out of the room.

"I can try to retrieve it, my lord!" Anne called after him.

Aylesbury stopped in his tracks, thinking, but did not turn back.

Anne continued. "If I stole it from you, what's to say I can't steal it back again?"

The nobleman whipped around. He glared at her as he thought about her comment. His bushy gray eyebrows shot up. "Do you even know where to look?"

She thought a moment and then went on. "I know Collin does not live with his father, but in a town not far from my home. It is a beginning . . . "

Edmond saw the twinkle of an idea brewing in Aylesbury's slate-colored eyes. It dawned on him that the nobleman was serious about this proposition. He stepped forward in protest. "Uncle, you cannot think to enlist the help of this—this—girl! She will try to escape the first moment—"

"Which is why you are going to go with her, Edmond. You shall be a captain to my men."

Anne frowned.

Dorsay jumped in. "There is little time for retrieving the map, your grace."

Aylesbury shook his head. "We have little choice."

Turning to Anne, he directed, "Girl, you will go with Captain Edmond, and you will retrieve what you have stolen."

Edmond objected again. "We still won't have the time we need to bring back the—"

Aylesbury cut in. "Whoever has it will soon be on their way to the Sword *and* the gold. You will have to go on from there when you have the King's Birthright." Turning to Anne, he added, "You, young woman, if you can help lead my men to Excalibur, you shall be pardoned for tonight's offense and will be rewarded in gold, as well."

"Do you mean Excalibur, *the sword*?"

Ignoring her question, Lord Aylesbury turned to Dorsay. "Besides, we will *all* be as good as dead if we don't find the Birthright soon. Dorsay, while you are at it, please make sure the manor guard is better prepared should something more dangerous than two thieves decide to pay us a future visit."

Shamefaced, Dorsay bowed and walked out of the room.

"So, my lord?" Anne implored, expecting an answer.

Without a response, Aylesbury turned and wrapped his arm around Edmond's shoulder, walking him toward a door and continuing to ignore Anne. "Come with me to my study, Edmond. We have much to cover before you can leave."

"Yes, uncle."

"So . . . no execution?" Anne said to their backs.

There was no response. The captain and the nobleman were deep in hushed conversation as they exited the room. Anne, her wrists and ankles still bound, followed them with anxious eyes, then glanced down at the ropes binding her.

"Great! So, shall I pack for a trip? Saddle a horse?"

The unresponsive voices faded beyond the door, then disappeared altogether when a sentry closed the oak door behind them with a heavy slam.

Anne was alone in the room.

"Uh . . . Hello? *Anybody*? Wouldn't you like to untie me?" she inquired to no one in particular.

CHAPTER 7

Wednesday – Daybreak
Highbridge

ANNE STOOD BESIDE THE GUARD Salgar's horse. Leather creaked around her as saddlebags were loaded onto horses in the damp semidarkness. She half listened to the clopping sound of hooves preparing to carry their riders out of the stable courtyard.

It had been an uncomfortable night. She had realized that there was no way she could possibly sleep while sitting on the small stool. She surveyed the room in the half-light of a candle left by one of the guards. Would the cold slate stones of the floor work? The movement of a small rodent scurrying across the floor had discouraged her from that option. With hands and feet bound, she had somehow managed to wiggle herself over to a banquet hall bench. It was wide enough to lie down on her back, but it was hard to even doze, worrying that she might toss and turn and fall from the bench. But eventually sleep arrived.

Now as she stood outside the manor she surveyed the entourage through gritty, half-awake eyes. Perkins and Salgar were a bit hungover and bruised after their encounter with the two shadows the night before, but were among the men in the company preparing to leave the manor.

Salgar required two tries to heave his large mass up and onto a small gray horse. Perkins, meanwhile, painfully lowered his helmet onto his bandaged head. He glared at Anne, who was now clothed in a red dress with white sleeves. It was actually a servant's uniform that had been borrowed from one of the manor's chambermaids.

Salgar glanced at his partner, then down at Anne. Her wrists were tied to the horn of the round man's saddle. "So, Perkins. Do yer think I should go for a ride and exercise the horse before we go out?"

"You wouldn't!" Anne, alarmed, looked up at the fat man.

Perkins smiled widely through brown teeth, most of them crafted of wood. "'Fraid of gett'n your clothes dirty, miss?"

Anne was getting fed up with the verbal jabs by the two guards. Swinging one leg upward, her foot caught the reins of Salgar's horse and gave them a hard pull. The gray mare, perhaps already bothered by the obese guard's weight, reared up on her hind legs, pulling Anne briefly into the air, while also causing Salgar to slide over the side to the ground, landing with a loud thump, his foot still caught in a stirrup. Anne scrambled back onto her feet.

She turned to Perkins, sneering threateningly, as if to ask whether he wanted to continue prodding her. Timidly, he coaxed his own mare several steps away from Salgar's position. Three other guards were watching the scene, chuckling among themselves as they prepared to depart.

Edmond seemed to appear from nowhere, walking up to Anne. "Ah, I see you've met Salgar, then." He looked around. "And this fellow who seems to have had better luck mounting his horse would be Perkins?"

"Yes, Captain." There was resignation in Salgar's voice as he extracted his foot from the stirrup and maneuvered his mass to a standing position. "Just looking for something I dropped, sir."

Edmond untied the leather strap affixing Anne to Salgar's saddle horn, leaving her wrists tied together. He led her with unexpected gentleness to a slender chestnut mare of her own, its reins fastened forward to a larger white stallion.

"Do you like the dress, miss?"

"I think I preferred my father's breeches to this."

"You know, I don't think you ever told us your name."

"Not sure it would have mattered when you asked it last night. It's Anne. Anne du Lac."

"Well, Anne, you may call me Captain Edmond."

"Am I to be tied the entire time, Captain?"

"No. I think in that red dress, we've little to worry about how far you will wander. The color can be seen from quite a distance."

Edmond unsheathed a knife at his side and cut the rope binding her wrists, holding out both arms to assist her and nodding at the saddle on her horse. Anne snubbed his offer and mounted the horse on her own. *Much easier the second time*, she thought. The captain shrugged and turned.

"Mount up!" he shouted to the troop.

Edmond slid into the fancy studded saddle on the white stallion. He prodded his horse forward, motioning Anne to ride at his side. The company left the estate in formation through the large wooden gates at a brisk walk.

Anne looked at Edmond on her left. "Do you really believe the sword of King Arthur still exists?"

He nodded. "Your friend took the one thing that could show us where to find it."

"And your lord needs it?"

Edmond stared at her for a few moments and then at the trail ahead. He said nothing.

She pressed on. "He needs it for succession to the throne?"

"First a thief, and now a theorist?"

"Ahhh, but the lord promises reward for helping you find Excalibur. I think I can fit it together. The king died recently without an heir."

She watched the captain to see whether the statement hit home, but his face showed no emotion whatsoever.

He looked at her. "Actually, he had two illegitimate heirs."

"And the nobility is all up in arms about which one gets the kingdom, Lord Aylesbury or the second heir? Is that right?"

Edmond went silent again.

Anne took this as confirmation of her theory. Emboldened, she continued.

"So, all we have to do is steal from a thief, find a mythical sword, and make a king, right?"

Edmond still did not reply.

Anne twisted in her saddle to examine the team on the journey. She gazed at Salgar, balancing uneasily in a saddle that seemed undersized for his large frame. She heard Perkins belch after a taking a good gulp from his water skin, which she was certain did not contain water.

"Something wrong?" Edmond asked her.

"No. No problem at all."

CHAPTER 8

The sun had climbed above the horizon, and speckles of light flashed across the ground through the leafy canopy above. The troop was well out of sight of the estate, and the horses had slowed to a steady walk. Twisting in his saddle, Edmond surveyed his company of soldiers. Two riders back he saw Salgar, whose large body was obviously sensing the heat of the day. He watched the guardsman wipe his forehead with a soiled hankie and take a swig of water from his water skin.

Dorsay, meanwhile, led his horse around the group, an anxious look on his face. He scanned the ground without blinking.

"Tracks, Captain," he said, pointing to the side.

The captain reined his stallion to a stop, his gaze following Dorsay's indication of an area of trampled underbrush. Signaling the rest of the party to halt, Edmond snapped his head toward Anne.

"You said he was alone!"

"Yes. It was just me and him."

"I think not. Come with me."

Edmond dismounted for a closer look. Stooping, he began to follow the trail of trampled undergrowth. Dorsay moved to his side, crouching to better see the tracks. Anne also alighted and followed.

Moments later, Edmond, Dorsay, and Anne were in a small clearing, obscured by brush and foliage from the horses and men on the path. In the center of the glade were the warm remains of a campfire.

"Do you know if he had plans to meet anyone?" Edmond asked Anne.

"Not until he returned the box of gold to its owner." Uncertainty now crept into her voice. "You must believe me."

She scanned the ground, seeing foot- and hoofprints scattered around. And a broken club.

"It looks as though a small army's been through here," the captain murmured to himself.

"At least seven mounted men, maybe one or two more, and a struggle." Dorsay paced around the camp, walking on the balls of his feet with a honed grace. He looked at Anne. "Our thief has either been taken or killed."

"I find it easy to hate him," Anne remarked. "But I don't think he deserved death."

"Edmond, you should see this." Dorsay knelt down once more.

The trio huddled over a mass of dark mud by a tree. There were several hoofprints, but one set was deeper than the others, filled with what appeared to be black water.

Dorsay gingerly touched the liquid in one of the deep prints with the fingers of one hand. He withdrew his hand and held it up for the others to examine. The color made it clear to all that the prints were not filled with water. They were filled with blood.

"Perhaps he *is* dead, then," Edmond said.

Anne's anxiety about her situation was quickly turning to worry. If Collin *was* dead, she would no longer be useful to Aylesbury and his men.

Dorsay cut in. "It's not the blood that's important here." He traced the shape of a horseshoe print. "A very large horse made this print. A very heavy one."

Anne shrugged. "Maybe one of them rode a draft horse."

Dorsay shook his head. "With those shoes, I'd say the horse is a courser. A huge destrier. And with a pack of men, that means much."

Edmond's eyes turned away. "Lambert?"

Dorsay nodded slowly. "I have no doubt that it was Lambert."

"What is a destrier?" Anne inquired.

"A very rare and very large warhorse," Edmond replied. "They aren't used much any longer." He turned again to Dorsay. "How far ahead?"

"Hard to say. Between the fire and the chaos, I'd say probably six or seven hours."

Edmond turned back to Anne.

"Go back to the horses," he said.

Anne nodded and silently turned to leave.

Edmond crouched down with Dorsay to survey the hoofprints. "Lambert, again! Why can't I get that creature out of my life?"

"Sometimes things are just meant to be. That's what I think, Captain," Dorsay consoled Edmond.

"He wants the throne. There can be no doubting that. If he had it, at least we would have peace rather than chaos, for surely the present disarray will continue until the throne is again occupied. But I'm certain we will see tyranny from the sovereign if Lambert ascends. The people just do not realize how evil that man can be."

Edmond thought back to his youth. He and Lambert had been close in their early years. Born into privilege, both were competitive fighters, but Lambert could not accept a loss of any kind. As cadets at the military academy in Delney, both were trained in the art of war. But while Edmond mastered swordsmanship, Lambert became known as a violent handler of such brutal weapons as the ball and chain, poleax, and pommel. In the course of one battle-training exercise, another cadet died at the end of Lambert's poleax. Some said it was an accident, while others whispered that it had happened purposefully. Following the tragic event, Lambert became known quietly among the students as "the Butcher of Delney," a name that hounded him even after graduation from the school.

After college, Edmond and Lambert went separate ways. Upon the accidental death of Edmond's parents, Edmond was taken under the wing of his uncle, Lord Aylesbury. Over the last five years, the childless Aylesbury had come to think of Edmond as if the young captain were his own son. Tales of Lambert filtered back to Edmond from time to time, and it slowly became apparent from the Butcher's evil exploits that the man had become more ruthless and cruel, in every way living up to his nickname.

"Er, Captain? Shouldn't we be on our way?" Dorsay's voice wrenched Edmond back from his memories. The captain stared at his trusted friend as if he were just waking from a dream.

"Yes, Dorsay, we must move on. More than that, we must reach Excalibur and the treasure before Lambert. Let's get back to our men."

CHAPTER 9

Wednesday – Midday
Woodlands Due East of Highbridge

AFTER LEAVING EDMOND AND DORSAY, Anne made her way back through the trampled path within the dense forest growth. Looking ahead, she realized the rest of the party of horsemen had not noticed her coming. She looked back over her shoulder and saw Edmond and Dorsay still kneeling in whispered discussion, their backs turned toward her.

Anne altered her route a little and took a casual step off the path into the brush at her right and stopped. After a minute of silence, she took one more step off the pathway. Glancing around and listening intently, she confirmed that she had not been spotted and fled in a direction parallel to the horse path, running through several shrubs with scattered muffled gasps when the branches scratched at her.

More than once she was waylaid as the hem of her red dress caught on brambles. She stopped and yanked the hem upward and began running again.

Suddenly she heard shouts behind her, though the words were indiscernible amid the louder sounds of branches breaking underfoot and bushes scraping against her side. Red-faced from the exertion, she ran harder, keeping her eyes on the ground to avoid obstacles.

Then Anne realized that the loud shouting had changed direction, even though she had been running in a more or less straight line. Shifting her eyes up from the forest floor, she thought she could see running shadows through the dense foliage ahead. From the horse path on her left, she could hear loud galloping as her pursuers repositioned themselves.

She thought she heard the voice of Salgar calling to other riders. “The brush is thick, but she’ll be easy t’ spot in that swell red dress, men!”

Now sighting people and not just shadows through the brush ahead, Anne stopped dead in her tracks and searched frantically for options.

She held her breath and cocked her head to the right. She heard nothing threatening, then pivoted to her right, changing her direction so that now she was perpendicular to the horse path, carrying her away from both riders and runners. Running again, she tore at the laces binding her red dress and gradually peeled off pieces of clothing, first the bodice, then the skirt and interlaced top. As each piece came off, she stooped and shoved it beneath the underbrush.

Finally, she was left running through the forest in a short, cream-colored underdress and her boots, hoping that leaving the red dress behind would somehow ease her escape.

Changing direction again, she suddenly came to a steep incline and sailed over the crest, much too late to stop. Before landing, her boot caught on a tree root and she flew forward, landed on her side, then rolled down the lower part of the slope to the bottom of a gully.

Anne stood up very slowly and pressed on different parts of her body with her hands. She felt a little soreness here and there, but no real pain. Nothing felt broken, so she began to dust off some of the leaves, ferns, and dirt she had acquired on her descent.

She heard Salgar's voice again, distant but clear. "I found 'er red dress, Captain!" Then came the far-away sound of a dog barking. She knew there were no dogs in the troop. *So where did that come from?* She decided it was a wild dog, probably foraging for food, not an unusual occurrence in the area. As long as it remained away from the area, she wouldn't worry about it.

She couldn't stop any longer so she gave up dusting off the leaves and dirt. *Oh well. I'll blend in.*

Anne started off again, away from Salgar's voice and the gully. Her breathing was getting heavier and heavier, and she stumbled again, her body tiring. But voices could still be heard. *Oh, just give up, will you?*

As she wiped sweat and dirt off her face, Anne noticed the tree canopy towering over her. An idea came to her, and she tried to snatch a large frond from a fern. The greenery, however, gave her a hard time, as if it were rooted in stone.

Anne gave it a good pull. Nothing happened. She twisted it. Nothing. She bit at the stem, sputtering at the taste. Still no movement. As she was wiping her mouth with the back of her hand, she spotted an identical frond on the ground.

Grabbing it, she began to walk backward, sweeping the ground to eliminate her tracks in the dry leaves and earth. Finally, stuffing the fern frond into the string belt of her shift, she began to climb a large tree, nimbly using every available foothold to carry her higher into its branches.

CHAPTER 10

It was the hottest point of a very hot day. *It's always this way in the early afternoons of summer*, Edmond thought, as several men on foot surveyed the ground in front of them for tracks, some carrying pieces of Anne's dress. Perkins and Dorsay were leading the horses. Edmond was atop the white stallion. The entourage was directly below the tree that Anne had climbed minutes before.

"Salgar," Edmond said. "Go survey the top of the ridge over there."

"Begging your pardon, sir," the fat man said. "Tis an awful climb off horseback."

Edmond frowned. "I seem to recall this being a penance for your failure last night, Salgar, not a holiday."

Dorsay squinted at Salgar through one eye, his face beginning to show an anger that was feared throughout the troop. "You'd better move along or you'll have an awful way of it on horse *and* foot after I'm done with you, Salgar," he growled.

The rest of the men within hearing range began to look very interested in nonexistent tracks, trying hard to avoid staring at the scene.

Salgar fumbled with a piece of his armor, his face beet red as he turned and began walking briskly toward the ridge.

Dorsay stared hard at the captain. An understanding passed between them, then he led his horse away from the tree. "I'll take the area to the west," he said.

Edmond nodded and led his horse in the opposite direction.

Above the group, Anne looked down from her perch in the tree, watching Salgar as he turned back toward the troop. "Perkins! This way!" Salgar called.

Anne waited. It was now very quiet below her.

For the first time, in the stillness, she began to wonder what her parents were feeling and doing in her absence. Had they called on neighbors for help? Were they searching for her? She missed them terribly. But somehow she knew down deep that the only way she could ever escape from her situation would require that she act on her own. *But what action?* For the moment, she kept herself very still, listening for sounds of any living thing that might hamper her escape.

After about fifteen minutes, Anne decided she would slip out of the tree and move away from it in a different direction. At this point, she was straddling a large branch, and she swung one leg up and over it to reposition herself for the descent. As she did so, her boot snapped a small branch, which fell to the ground below. Almost instantly, the dog she earlier heard yapping in the distance came running up to the base of the tree and began barking up at her. *Just what I need right now.*

She held herself absolutely still, hoping the animal would get bored enough to give up its quest. And in fact, the dog did stop barking, but it kept its eyes fixed squarely on Anne sitting above, as if expecting something from her.

She knew she needed to steer the animal away from the tree. *But how?*

Inching her hand along the branch she was sitting on, Anne grabbed a thin branch and snapped it off. Hoping to distract the dog's attention away from her, she threw the twig as far as she could. As it arced to the ground, the branch scraped other foliage and the sound caused the dog to turn its head and follow the sound of its descent.

The branch hit the ground. She watched the dog. Nothing happened for a minute or two. The dog had gone quiet, possibly considering whether its hunt for Anne would ever yield anything to eat.

I'll never get away from here if that creature doesn't move on. She surveyed the area around the tree. There was no sight of Edmond's men. No sound of horses, either.

Then she heard it.

Another wild dog was barking not far beyond the stand of trees she was in. Looking down, she watched in amazement as the animal waiting below turned from her tree, and taking a few steps backward, angled its ears toward the distant barking. After a moment's hesitation, the dog below her barked twice and then bounded away toward the sound of the other animal, disappearing from sight within thirty seconds.

Anne's shoulders drooped in relief, and she pressed her head back against the trunk of the tree. Closing her tired eyes, she decided to allow a few more minutes before making her next move.

About ten minutes later, two very scuffed and muddy legs adorned in even dirtier ladies' boots descended slowly from the tree. Anne jumped the last ten feet or so, landing clumsily on the ground. She stood up and straightened her shift, smoothing it down with her hands as if it were a proper dress. Then she turned to leave.

Ahead of her another thirty feet or so, she saw Edmond, waiting with the red dress over one arm.

I'm found out.

"Finally!" he said, a smile of self-satisfaction crossing his face, "I thought I might have to shoot you down."

Anne didn't miss a beat. She turned and bolted in the opposite direction, only to run right into Dorsay, who easily contained her kicking fury with one strong arm.

Edmond walked up to them, holding out the dress. "Please put this on."

"It's in tatters!" Anne said, immediately changing tactics. "I don't know who you think I am, but—"

Edmond was losing patience. "You are a thief and you *will* wear it no matter what the condition."

Looking from Edmond to Dorsay and back to Edmond, Anne snatched the dress from his arms and donned it.

"I don't know any more than what I've told you. If Collin is dead, then there is nothing more I can do or say."

Edmond stared at her for a moment. She wore the gaudy, now frayed, red dress over her filthy shift along with a sour look on her face.

"I cannot let the only link to the Sword and the gold simply go free." Edmond began tying a length of leather strap around her wrists.

She was led away, attached to the leash-like strap, which looked a little like the reins leading Edmond's horse. The similarity did not go unnoticed by Anne.

She watched as Edmond turned to Dorsay. "She has caused us to waste much time. They have a huge lead, and we will have to ride hard to catch them."

Mounting his horse, Dorsay turned to the troop. "We ride, men! Boyles, watch ahead."

"Sir!" said Jerra Boyles, a scout with eyes that glanced about in a restless fashion, absorbing everything. He galloped up to the head of the line of men, and then left them behind on his fast steed.

Anne was tied onto her horse's saddle, with her arms wrapped around its neck and her wrists bound together. Her horse was tethered to Edmond's by a long strap. All in all, it wasn't comfortable.

The rest of the company mounted up and they took off at a hard pace.

CHAPTER 11

Wednesday Night
A Forest Road East of Wedmore

THE SUN HAD SET LONG ago. The light that was left was fading into the cool purples of a cloudless night.

Edmond led the line of men, watching intently ahead. The troop's horses were moving at a fast walk as darkness descended and limited the visibility ahead.

Anne was still bound to her horse's neck. She turned her head toward the group and then toward Edmond, now riding next to her. This got her the view. It also got her a mouthful of the horse's mane. She tried to spit it out a few times, but several strands still stuck.

The captain noticed this little scene and smiled, almost respectfully. *Even hunched over and a filthy, sweaty mess, she seems a fearless girl.*

He leaned over and cleared the hair from her mouth for her. At first, Anne jerked her head back. Then she realized that he only wished to help. She lifted her chin slightly to allow him to clear it. Stubborn as she was, she was not without some grace. "Thank you," she said.

Edmond inclined his head, smiling. His eyes lingered on her.

Dorsay noticed this as he rode in beside Edmond. "Boyles found a day camp where they rested. I'd say they're three or so hours ahead. We've made good time, Edmond."

"Yes, we have. Good work."

"Good men. Which brings me to mention that we should make camp soon, sir."

"You are right, friend. And your reminder implies that we are very close to a good location—"

"We are. Twenty yards to the side," Dorsay cut in, pointing with his chin, then falling back to relay orders. "Men, halt!"

Edmond pulled up beside Anne's horse and dismounted. Stepping over to her, he pulled a knife from his belt and cut the rope tying her to the saddle, then walked away, neglecting to untie the rope that was binding her hands around the horse's neck.

When she finally managed to roll out of the saddle, she found herself swinging around in front of the horse, her face pushed up against the mare's jaw. The horse lowered its head in response to the extra weight of Anne pulling on its neck. All of this resulted in her face being pushed up against the mare's drooling mouth. Anne let out a short yelp.

Shocked, the horse proceeded to walk backward, dragging Anne along with it. With a grunt, and resisting the urge to gag, Anne managed to pull its head even lower and then slid her tied wrists over the horse's neck and head. Now, standing in front of a very relieved animal, she wiped the horse slobber off her face with a sleeve of her dress.

Salgar arrived on the scene, and before she could recover from her misadventure with her horse, he had looped a length of rope through her already-bound wrists and formed another leash.

"Now, there she is," he said aloud to no one, affecting a note of disgust in his voice. "Trying to escape ag'in are we? We'll have none of that, miss, if you please."

By a little after midnight the temperature had plunged, and the soldiers were huddled around a warm fire next to a large creek. One guard attempted to chew at his set of rations, a stringy salted meat. He was not succeeding very well and feared he would lose a tooth or two while trying. Another looked at his portion of meat and carefully slipped it behind him, onto the ground. Edmond and Dorsay chewed their own tasteless meat laboriously, as if taking some sort of medicine. Perkins drowned his bites with occasional gulps from his liquor stash. The sky had gone from purple twilight to pitch blackness except where the moon still hung, on its way toward the horizon.

Anne was seated alone at her own personal fire at the rear of the camp. Her legs and hands were bound in front of her, and she had little room to move. She prodded with both hands at the dried meat and cheese crumbles atop the flat rock next to her. *Enough of this! I must be free of these straps.*

She managed to gain her footing and stand upright. Hopping a few inches at a time, she worked her way toward the larger fire.

One soldier told a joke and the rest of the company erupted in laughter, with Edmond laughing along with them. Anne tapped the captain on the shoulder and he turned with a start. "What?"

"I'd like to fetch my own food," said Anne.

Edmond eyed her up and down. "Men," he said aloud, "she's going to fetch her own food, she says." The soldiers all stared, smirking.

"A knife, please." Anne said.

"No, I don't think I can give you one."

"Well a stretch of rope and a pan will do, then."

"Watch out, men," Salgar said. "She'll swat you in yer sleep, she will." The soldiers laughed.

Edmond decided to be kinder to her and handed her a metal pan and a length of thin rope. Anne waited, expecting the captain to free her wrists. Nothing happened.

"Very well, I can do it with my hands tied."

"I hope so," said Edmond, "because I cannot untie them." He then loosened the binding around her ankles enough to free her to walk in a slightly hobbled way, but not enough that she could run.

He watched as she went to the edge of the creek, where she squatted down. She worked the length of rope between her fingers, knotting it here, stretching it there, to form a mesh net with ends. Then she stepped into the moonlit river water, hunched over, and dropped her bound hands below the water line. Her red dress was tucked between her knees. She looked like some strange sort of gypsy.

Anne waited patiently, shifting her weight like a cat about to pounce.

Abruptly, she smiled and jerked the ends of the rope upward, but this caused her to slip and she fell backward into the water, soaking nearly every inch of herself.

Huddled by the fire, the fifteen men watching her roared with laughter, grateful for a distraction from their awful rations. But in her lap, a very large fish bounded about in the small makeshift net.

She pulled herself up, dripping river mud and water.

Stumbling a little, Anne hobbled proudly past the soldiers, some still rolling on the ground with laughter.

Reaching her smaller campfire, Anne plunked the huge fish on her pan. The sizzling sound of the frying fish caused heads to turn, and as all eyes fixed on her, the laughter died out.

Fifteen minutes later, Anne, her dress still damp, sat on a rock with her back to the troop of soldiers. Some of them licked their lips as she ate a portion of the cooked fish. She smiled, wholly pleased with herself.

One of the men quietly stood, slipped away from the larger fire and approached her. Soon, almost all of the men were gathered around her little fire. Looking at their pleading expressions, she relented and apportioned all but two final pieces of the fish to each one.

Meanwhile, back at the main fire, Edmond was sitting with his only companion, Dorsay, who was trying to hold his laughter back and failing horribly.

Wiping her mouth with her sleeve, Anne squirmed to a standing position and made her way with the last pieces of fish over to Dorsay and then to Edmond, who accepted it, throwing his own meat away. He raised his piece of fish with both hands, as if to salute her. "Well done," he marveled, smiling.

CHAPTER 12

Thursday – Late Morning
East of Cheddar

ANNE RUBBED HER WRISTS ABSENTMINDEDLY. Now free of straps and altogether unbound, she still felt like she was a prisoner, which in fact she was. Several eyes kept a watch on her.

The day was cloudy as a weather front moved in from the open water several miles to the west. The company was continuing its manhunt, although the pace of the horses was a little slower due to the hilly terrain.

Ahead of the group were two figures on horseback coming rapidly toward them: Salgar and Perkins. Salgar was bouncing in his saddle as his galloping horse approached the train of men. Perkins rode up just behind him. They pulled to a halt directly in front of Edmond and Dorsay.

"Captain. Sir Dorsay. We found the tracks! You should know that one of them looks like a very large horse, maybe one of the old warhorses, sir. That could be the likes of—"

"Thank you, Salgar," Edmond cut him off.

"That's not all, sir," said Perkins. "There's some sort of burning ahead. Black smoke."

Salgar nodded in agreement. "Something large, about three or four miles or so to the east."

"That sounds like the monastery at Wells, Captain," said Dorsay.

"That means our culprits are not far away at all." Edmond turned to Dorsay. "Everyone ready up. We go at once."

With Edmond and Dorsay leading the pack, the company rode in the direction of the monastery.

Black smoke was obscuring the sky like a diseased cloud. Though most of the monastery was intact, a large granary adjacent to the abbey's main building was in flames, its thatched roof already consumed, and no one was trying to extinguish the blaze.

A bearded giant of a man in heavy armor sat astride a very large horse that was restlessly pacing between the fire and the monastery. The man's name was Lambert, but he was known as the Butcher of Delney, and from every pore in his tanned skin he radiated evil.

There were several similarly armored men on each side of him, holding lighted torches and forming a sort of runway for his massive warhorse as it stepped back and forth. At first glance, they looked like small men on ponies. But on a second look, it became obvious that they were of average build. The Butcher, by contrast, was a huge man on a horse of gargantuan proportions.

Inside the monastery, several monks were huddled behind shuttered windows. They ranged in age from young to ancient. Most were peering out of small windows and portals, looking forlornly at their burning food stores. Others were piling furniture against a large entry door. Near the entrance door was the elderly Father Antony, pacing back and forth.

On the outside of the door, arms crossed over his chest, was Brother Kromm. His legs were set wide apart, his stance firm and imposing.

"Brothers! Brothers!" the Butcher said loudly, intending his words for those within. "I come seeking your help."

"We cannot give you what you ask." Kromm's tone was firm.

The Butcher's right-hand man was Lurch, a wiry person with less brains than teeth, of which there remained very few. Lurch was astride his own horse at the Butcher's side.

"Did he just address me as 'your highness?'" the Butcher asked Lurch in a voice intended for Kromm.

"He did not, m'lord," confirmed Lurch, a smirk creeping across the cheeks scarred from backroom fights.

"Hmmm. That's what I thought," the Butcher said, holding out a hand to another of his henchmen. He was handed a burning torch. In his other hand, he held the red box with the gold dragon that Anne had retrieved from Aylesbury's manor house. He pretended to be interested in the torch's wrappings, examining every inch of it as he spoke.

He lifted the box slightly. "If you do not hand over the stone disk guarded by your order, every one of you will have to answer for it, monk."

The Butcher led his massive horse over to one edge of the monastery building. Like the food stores, it was topped with a thatched roof. He held the bright torch high in the air just far enough away from the straw on the roof to prevent starting another fire, but close enough to threaten a disaster.

"I already have much to answer for, letting you enter these grounds," Brother Kromm said.

"Father Antony!" called the Butcher. "Come out and come with us and we will spare your simple brethren. Do you not wish to save your order?"

He pointed to the blazing fire that was once the granary building. "Already your cowardice will make all here starve in the winter," he continued.

"Father Antony will not come," Kromm said, his voice firm yet somehow peaceful, as he stood up against the monster of a man in front of him. "We are all prepared to face the hereafter, if it is necessary," added the monk.

The Butcher began to pace his horse in front of the monastery, back and forth like a restless tiger, his torch still held high. "Father Antony!" he called again, ignoring Brother Kromm's words. No response came from within the building. He waited half a minute. His anger built. Still there was no response.

"Then you will all burn!" he shouted.

The Butcher positioned himself where he could be clearly seen through an opening beside the entrance door. He slowly lifted the torch higher and closer to the roof, and the dry reeds began to smolder, the smell of smoke wafting through the roof and downward to where Father Antony was standing on the inside.

"Wait!" Father Antony shouted. "I am coming!"

The Butcher withdrew his torch from the roof's edge, staring intently at the door.

There was a sound to his right. He turned his head in time to see a very rotund man, Father Antony, emerge from a cellar door in the ground beside the monastery.

The monk's cheeks were puffy and red below wide, brown eyes. The top of his head was a shining dome, his trimmed brown hair falling away on all sides. Sweat was rolling off his forehead in the heat of the day. The holy man's brown robes, gathered around his waist with a braided leather cord, were unusually untidy and spotted with ink. He timidly walked to a point on the ground about ten feet away from the massive warhorse.

The Butcher looked down at him. "Where is the stone?" he asked.

The monk said nothing.

"The Brothers' Burden! I want it! Where is that stone?!" the Butcher demanded again, his voice a level or two louder, anger exploding in his voice.

His whole body beginning to shake, Father Antony replied in a broken, soft voice. "The Brothers' Burden is a myth. I cannot believe you would come here for the sake of legends and wives' tales."

"*Do you think I am here to play*?" the Butcher said, now raising the volume of his voice. He angrily turned and hurled his torch onto the building roof, and a patch began to burn.

He barked an order to a henchman. "Hand me another torch!"

"Please, spare the abbey!" Father Antony pleaded.

The Butcher looked down at him. "Father, you might be able to save it yet, if you answer me now. *Where is the stone called the Brothers' Burden*?"

"I beg of you," replied a weary Father Antony. "We do not have it. The stone was stolen from us years ago."

Inside the cellar from which Father Antony had emerged, the shy Brother Mallory was sitting on a wooden crate with his back to the commotion above, shivering and praying, his eyes squeezed shut. He was a wiry young man whose face probably would not need to touch a razor for another few years. In his hands he clutched a carved stone disk wrapped in red cloth. The Brothers' Burden.

Outside, the Butcher prepared to throw a second torch onto the roof. "It is a pity that you will not take me seriously," he said to the monk below him.

"I studied its markings before it was taken," said Father Antony.

This stopped the Butcher from heaving his torch.

"Take me, and I can help you on your search."

"Father Antony!" Kromm cried in shock.

"Take me. But you must leave the monastery, now," Father Antony continued, his eyes burning with a certain anger as he stared at the Butcher. Turning to Kromm, he ordered quietly, "You will take my place while I am gone."

The Butcher inclined his head slightly, a signal to one of his henchmen, who immediately broke formation with an extra horse trailing his own. The guard approached the monk and offered the reins.

"A wise decision, monk."

The rotund monk was directed to mount up.

"There's nothing wise about it. I have no choice."

After several tries and a helping heave by the closest henchman, Father Antony finally sat in the saddle. His rolls of fat bulged over the edges.

"Let us go, then," the monk suggested, "and leave the order out of it." He looked up at the fire spreading across the roof.

"M'lord!" came a sudden call. All eyes turned toward a man riding bareback up to the monastery at a furious speed. The middle-aged man looked like a beggar, his clothes patched and filthy. An untidy mop of a beard was swinging below his chin.

The Butcher turned to the apparition. "What is it, Hunder?"

Hunder slowed only when he neared the Butcher. There was a long knife stuck into his rope belt, contrasting with an otherwise perfect image of poverty. His voice sounded like a series of gasps more than words.

"M'lord," he continued. "Fifteen men and a woman, at full speed toward us, and they wear Aylesbury's colors."

"They're so desperate," Lurch interrupted, "they be recruitin' women now."

The henchmen laughed, but the Butcher waved the laughter to a stop. He was all business. "They must have followed the thief somehow. How far?"

"About ten minutes away, m'lord. Maybe less."

"Good work, Hunder." The Butcher reached into a side pocket and threw the lookout a small gold coin. Hunder caught it like a frog catching insect prey. He bit into it with his wooden teeth and slid it into an already well-laden pouch under his dirty tunic.

The Butcher leaned over toward Lurch and whispered directions that brought a smile.

"Yes, m'lord." Lurch turned to the other henchmen. "To the road, men!" To Father Antony, he said, "Come, monk. Time to go."

On his way out, Lurch grabbed the reins of the monk's horse, bringing it to a trot behind them. Father Antony held the saddle pommel tightly, fearful of falling from the horse with every footfall.

The Butcher and Hunder were the only two left behind.

"Hunder, I want you to scout ahead of the party."

"Yes, m'lord."

Hunder and his lithe horse sprinted ahead, easily catching up to and passing the group's horses.

The Butcher was now the only one left. Looking at Kromm, still planted firmly in front of the monastery door, he raised his torch and smiled confidently, as if silently boasting to the monk before him. Without so much as a word, he lit the rim of the thatched roof, marching his horse under the overhang around the building to burn more and more of the dried straw. Gasps came from inside as the huddled monks saw more of their life go aflame.

Then, like an exclamation point at the end of a sentence, the Butcher ended the encounter by throwing the torch up and onto the roof before he turned his massive horse and galloped off behind his men.

Immediately, most of the monks emerged with buckets and bedpans and ran for the monastery's well.

CHAPTER 13

EDMOND AND HIS MEN BROKE through the tree line surrounding the valley and descended upon the cluster of buildings under a murky sky.

As they burst through the haze, the horsemen took in the sight of the fire and the monks trying in vain to extinguish the flames on the roof of the abbey.

Edmond, coughing from the heavy smoke, was already dismounting as his stallion halted in front of Kromm. Dorsay pulled his mount to a stop beside Edmond seconds later.

"The scoundrels," said Kromm. "They were just here!"

Dorsay did not hesitate. "Edmond, if they were here only moments ago, this is our opportunity to overtake them and the map."

"How many, Brother?" asked the captain.

"Eight, I think, including the one they called the Butcher."

Edmond was clearly conflicted. "Without our help, their abbey will be lost," he said to Dorsay.

"A few can help here," suggested Dorsay. "Captain, let me lead the others. The Butcher's gang are only eight. We will be a good match for strength."

Edmond glanced at the burning stores, then the abbey, then back to Dorsay.

"Go, and be safe, my friend."

Dorsay remounted his horse, which was already prancing about, seemingly in anticipation. "I will have that stone map for you before nightfall, Edmond." He turned to his men, "Boyles! Salgar! Perkins! Take up a bucket and help them put out the fire!"

Then he turned his horse and led the others away, galloping toward the distant hills.

Edmond returned focus to the crisis at hand. The monks, now joined by the guardsmen, were passing buckets of well water hand-to-hand in a line. But the fire was harsh. He saw a frail, elderly monk fall from a ladder. The bucket that he was lifting hit the ground first, splintering and splashing water where it was least needed. Two other monks ran to help their fallen brother, diverting manpower from fighting the blaze.

"Let me help against the fire," Anne offered.

Salgar heard this between passing buckets. He shook his head and called to Edmond, "She'll try to escape ag'in, sir!"

"You need more people helping rather than watching me," she countered.

Salgar opened his mouth to argue, but was stayed when Edmond lifted his hand to him. "This is different from the woods. We could catch her in this valley even if she were gone an hour." Motioning Salgar to continue passing buckets, Edmond moved to untie Anne.

He turned to Anne, squinting one eye in a mild warning. "And if you try to escape, you'll also be wearing a harness for the rest of our journey."

Untied, and with a sour glance at Edmond, Anne ran for a bucket and took the place of the fallen monk on the ladder, delivering up pails of water to the thatched roof.

By late afternoon, the fire had finally been extinguished. Smoke and steam wafted throughout a scene of near devastation. Half of the abbey's roof was still intact, but the rest was charred and spotted with small holes. The food storehouse had been leveled to a pile of smoldering ash.

Edmond, accompanied by his three men, were in the abbey's great hall. They talked quietly as they worked to bandage and treat the monk that had fallen from his ladder, plus another dozen or so monks who had been either injured or overcome by the smoke.

Anne was outside with several other monks, helping to clear rubble and debris and to move some furniture that had been saved back into the abbey. She saw a dazed elderly monk slowly entering the abbey with a large bucket filled with water and dashed to his side to relieve him of his burden.

"Where should I take this?" she asked.

The monk smiled gratefully and gestured toward a kitchen in the depths of the monastery. The building was laid out like the letter **T** with the entry at the base. She lugged the bucket inside along the entry corridor, water occasionally sloshing over the pail's rim. A smoky haze lingered in the air, but it was no longer dangerously thick. Still, she could not stop her frequent coughing. She stumbled and the bucket sloshed a substantial amount of water on her, soaking the front of her tattered red dress. *Oh just wonderful!*

At the end of the entry corridor she turned left to the end where she found the kitchen and set the water bucket down before returning back down the hallway toward the main entrance. As she walked, she attempted to wring water out of sections of the dripping dress.

Then Anne heard loud coughing coming from the opposite end of the hallway. She walked past the main entrance corridor and continued down the hallway. She passed room by simple room, looking curiously into each one for the source of the sound. One large room held a line of straw beds laid side by side. The next room was a storehouse of raw goods in burlap bags, mainly flax and grain. In the next room, she saw a shirtless figure on a sickbed, silhouetted against the light pouring in through an open window. He coughed again, and she entered the room.

When her eyes adjusted to the shadows, she gasped audibly.

"Collin!"

Weary and pale, he opened his eyes, which began rolling upward as soon as he recognized Anne. Near to fainting in shock, Collin quickly drew a woolen blanket up to his neck, seemingly motivated more by fear than modesty.

"Anne? Oh no, I'm hallucinating again." He clamped his eyes shut and called out, "Brother Owen! Brother Owen!"

Anne was now really angry. "Collin, do you have any idea what you did?"

"Oh, Mother Mary, full of grace . . . "

"You'd better ask the good Lord to come and take you now, before I finish with you!" said Anne, her hand swatting uncontrollably at Collin, who squirmed to the farthest corner of the small bed.

"Stop, Anne!" he pleaded. "I'm already on my deathbed!"

She stopped, as if to evaluate his claim. "Look at my wounds, the blood I've lost," he said, without providing any evidence that Anne could see.

The slightest of smiles could then barely be seen on his face. "Oh, nice dress you've on. A bit damp though, isn't it?"

Anne's anger continued to rise. "I'll make sure you lose much more than blood, Collin Rogers. Where's the red box you stole?"

"Aye, I opened the box. No gold, nothing but a stone disk. They took it. They took the box!" Collin said, his voice lowering to a near whisper, as if he were admitting a deep secret.

"Who are '*they*'? The Butcher and his gang?"

She moved closer to him to better hear his answer, brushing against his side. He yelped in pain. "You're on my bloody wound, woman! Stay back!"

She bounded back a step but recognized an advantage she didn't have a moment ago.

"Oh, sorry . . ." she said with a sly smile. "Tell me who took the stone . . . and I shan't do it again."

His voice went to a lower whisper. "You're talking about the bloody Butcher. Keep it down!"

"He's long gone," she offered. "Did he hire you?"

"No, it was some fellow named Cors. Older, soldier type. I was supposed to meet him off the south road. The Butcher bounded in from out of nowhere and took the bloody box before givin' me this," he pointed toward the wound. "He said he was dropping me here to die, but I think he wanted to impress the monks with his ruthlessness."

"You won't die," said Anne. "But you'll wish you had when all's said and done."

She spotted a large soft leather bag in a corner near the bed. She went to it and opened it for a good look.

"What are you doing?"

"Thieving from a thief, I suppose."

"Those clothes are mine!"

"Not anymore. Good-bye, Collin. Not to worry. When I get back home, I'll make sure your father knows where you are. I'm sure he's wondering what his kind and honest and hardworking son has been doing and where he's been."

"You tell him about this, Anne, and you're still going to owe him every penny! You hear me? Every pen—"

Anne slapped him hard across the face. Physically weak, Collin was unable to resist without pain as Anne summoned great strength gained from years of swimming on the open water. She picked up a length of bandage lying nearby on the floor and, holding him down with an elbow, tied his wrists together. "I'm not as cruel as I'd like to be, Collin Rogers. But we are going to have to work on some sort of payment plan for your getting me into this mess. And I know just where to start!"

He cringed as she turned and left the room.

Fifteen minutes later, Anne emerged from an adjacent cell wearing Collin's breeches and jacket. She walked briskly past Collin's room, gesturing like she was brushing dirt off both hands, a wide smile on her face.

"Anne!" he called as he saw her pass, unable to move without great pain. Inside the cell, Collin was lying on the straw bed, his hands now bound behind his back. "Anne!" he tried again, to no avail.

As she neared the entrance door to the monastery, Salgar stepped out of a side room and confronted Anne. Her smile disappeared.

"I knew you would try escapin' ag'in. I jes' knew it!"

"Do I look like I'm running from here?" she asked directly as he grabbed her by the shoulders. She struggled briefly, but capitulated quickly as she was dragged down the hallway by the large man's brute strength.

A minute later, they emerged into the still-smoky air of the courtyard.

"Found 'er, Cap'n," he called to Edmond, who was seated against the building, attending to a wounded monk. The captain's expression said he was unimpressed.

"She wasn't missing. One of the brothers said she was taking water into the kitchen. You can let her go, Salgar."

"See?" Anne cocked her head toward Salgar as he begrudgingly released her.

"Er . . . I'll see to the horses then, sir," he mumbled under his breath as he began to walk off.

Edmond turned to Anne, now standing quietly to one side. His glance swept her from head to toe. "It does look like something's missing, doesn't it? Something red, perhaps?"

She straightened her trousers with a stubborn expression as Brother Kromm walked up with a cup and white cloth for bandaging.

"I can take it from here, Captain," said the holy man.

Edmond rose as Kromm took his place beside the wounded monk, offering up the cup of water.

"Why would a bunch of rogues attack your brotherhood?" the captain asked the monk, pretending to know a lot less than he did.

"Perhaps they wanted some sort of food for a journey. Who knows?" replied Kromm as he continued tending to the wounded.

"Food? But they took one of your brothers!"

"Ransom, revenge. There can be many reasons for such evil works," Kromm offered.

Anne stepped back as the scout, Jerra Boyles, briskly walked up. "Beggin' yer pardon, Cap'n. I think you should see this," Boyles said.

Boyles was trailing a leather leash at the end of which was Brother Mallory.

"Young Mallory . . . " Kromm said, frowning.

"He was tryin' to hide in the woods to the east, Cap'n. Scoutin' or desertin', I'm not sure. He doesn't seem to speak."

Kromm quickly entered the conversation at Mallory's side, taking the youth's arm in his. "Many brothers take a vow of silence. It is not unusual here. Come inside, Brother Mallory. No doubt you are exhausted."

"He was carryin' this," Boyles added, producing a medium-sized dark leather satchel. Turning it upside down, he emptied the contents onto a crate. Out came scrolls and something heavy bound by a crimson cloth.

Kromm moved to take the items, but Boyles stepped between the holy man and the crate. He lifted the heavy object and removed the red cloth carefully, exposing a carved stone disk, about the size of a hand.

Seeing a dragon symbol carved into the stone, Anne said, "Captain, that's the same symbol that was on the box at your uncle's home."

Edmond nodded, shooting her a silencing look.

"Uh—we—that was stolen," she continued, then went silent.

"What games are you playing, monk?" Edmond testily asked Kromm.

"Games? I have not lied to you."

"And you have not been entirely truthful, either."

Kromm took another tack. "I thank you for your help, Captain. The fire is nearly out, and I think perhaps it is time you continued on your quest."

Edmond lifted one eyebrow questioningly. "Then you won't mind if we take these scrolls with us? And the stone?"

"You'll do nothing of the sort," Kromm said.

This had no effect on Edmond. The captain folded the red cloth carefully around the stone and placed it inside the bagful of scrolls which he heaved onto his shoulder.

"For the quest, Brother," he said. "We know about the king's treasury and the Sword."

Anne stepped in again. "It will be only a matter of days at the most before it is found, Brother. Who would you rather have find it first?"

Mallory, still held virtually motionless by Jerra Boyles, watched the tense interplay with his eyes. Then, suddenly no longer mute, the young man spoke up.

"Th-th-they're right, B-Brother," he stammered to Kromm.

"Well, look at that," Jerra Boyles interjected. "Yer vows of silence don't hold too strong, do they, now?"

Mallory looked even more ashamed, but Kromm kept his head.

"I'm afraid we cannot help you," he said to Edmond.

"Who will protect the Sword from the Butcher and his intentions?" Edmond replied.

Kromm paused for barely five seconds, thinking. "You would only use it for your own intentions," he said, shaking his head sadly. "Again, the answer must be no."

Edmond paused, fingering the bag of scrolls on his shoulder.

Anne spoke up, her voice settling into a persuasive tone. "They took a monk, and we can help. Please, Brother. Let us help."

Kromm stepped over to an overturned bucket, and using it for a seat, slowly sat down. He looked ten years older from the wear of the day. He stared first at Edmond, then at Anne, and with an audible sigh, finally turned to look at Mallory.

"Tell them, then, Mallory," he ordered the youth.

Mallory, who had been staring at the ground most of this time, turned his eyes up and locked them on Edmond's.

"F-F-Father Antony is the head of our order," he stammered. "He is the only one who knows all of the Sword's secrets."

"Which is why the Butcher wanted him," volunteered Edmond.

"And he gave up the secret to save you," Anne added, looking at Kromm.

Kromm was shaking his head as if already in mourning for Father Antony. "No, he is ready to die for that secret. He went with the Butcher to buy us time. They will come back soon enough."

Mallory jumped in. "E-even if he wanted to, F-F-Father Antony c-cannot find the Sword without the carved stone you placed in your shoulder bag. It is the Brothers' Burden."

"That's why you took it away from the abbey," said Edmond.

"I-I-I meant to t-take it to a m-m-monastery in France, f-far from the B-B-Butcher."

All eyes turned on Kromm, who pressed his lips together tightly, raised both shoulders as if in defeat, and then began to explain things to Edmond.

"As Arthur's final battle was approaching, the king asked one of his knights to deliver the Brothers' Burden to the Bishop of Canterbury, a holy man that the king believed could safeguard the location of his secret vault. The king knew that no single man could be trusted with the secret. So he had commissioned a loyal stone cutter to detail its location using three physical clues.

"The King's Birthright, which has been in the possession of your uncle's family over the generations, is one of them. Another is the stone disk in your bag, the Brothers' Burden, that the bishop entrusted to the head of our order and which has been passed down for centuries. And it has been our charge to safeguard it from the flawed hands of men who would use it for ill purposes."

"So the gold *is* real?" asked both Anne and Edmond at the same moment. They looked at each other as if unsure who would speak next. Her facial expression said that she would defer to him.

"Is the Sword real?" asked Edmond.

"Many legends surround them," Kromm replied. "But the Sword, and the vault, and the gold it contains, are all real."

Mallory laid a hand on the leather bag still resting on Edmond's shoulder. "V-V-Very real," he added. "One of these t-t-texts is the holy man's diary, and w-w-within, it d-details how he protected the S-S-Sword so that each g-generation could know how to keep on p-p-protecting it."

"Before we felt the need today to betray that history," said Kromm, a tone of regret in his voice.

Edmond handed the leather pouch back to Mallory. "Tell us more," he said gently.

Mallory hesitantly searched the pouch with one hand and brought out, once again, the flat stone, removing the red cloth in which it was wrapped.

"On one side it marks the oath the holy man t-t-took." Mallory held the stone up. The smooth surface was deftly carved in a strange language.

"The other side looks like a maze," said Anne.

"Yes, it's a map of a maze, of some sort," said Kromm. "We think it marks the location of the Lady's Chamber, where the Sword is kept with Arthur's treasury."

"You *think*?" asked Edmond. "Don't you know?"

"The head of the order trains his successor in the secrets of the Sword. Only Father Antony and his dead predecessors know all of it. Father Antony has not yet trained one of us."

Edmond brushed his hand over the shoulder bag. "Can we find the Sword with what we have here?"

"No. You would also need the King's Birthright. And Father Antony to decipher the engravings."

"Then our fates are intertwined," said Edmond, rising. "If you come with us, Brother Mallory, we might find Father Antony and deliver him safely home."

"And the Sword?" asked Kromm.

"The Sword will begin a new chapter in the kingdom's history," Edmond replied solemnly.

"We will help you," Kromm promised. "However, you must swear that the Sword will be returned to its holding when Lord Aylesbury achieves the throne."

"Aylesbury? What do you know—"

"Swear!"

"I swear it, Brother Kromm."

Anne again joined the conversation. "You sound as if the Sword will bring the end of the world."

"No," said Kromm. "But if the Sword gets into the wrong hands, you might wish for the end of the world."

At that moment, Salgar returned from the makeshift fire brigade with Edmond's and Anne's horses in tow. "We've done all we can here, Cap'n," he said. Turning to Brother Kromm, Salgar mentioned that the storehouse was beyond saving.

Looking to the sky in supplication, Kromm said, "We will rebuild. The ashes will be spread among the new budding crop."

Edmond and Anne mounted their horses. Salgar went to assemble the others and fetch a horse for Brother Mallory.

"We ride now to join Dorsay," said Edmond. "Thank you, Brother Kromm."

And away they galloped, Salgar, Mallory and the remainder following behind.

A tear welled up in one of Brother Kromm's eyes as he watched them get smaller and smaller in the distance. *And the Lord be with you. For you will certainly need His protection.*

CHAPTER 14

Early Thursday Evening
A Field Road Southwest of Wells

THE DUST REACHED HIGH INTO the air, obscuring almost everything behind them on the wide path as Edmond, Boyles, Anne, Brother Mallory, Salgar, and Perkins rushed through the hilly countryside. Anne was unbound, but her horse was tethered to Edmond's steed, so she still had nowhere to run.

Even at a full gallop, Boyle's sharp eyes caught an early glimpse of something at the base of a hill directly in front of the group. He pointed it out to Edmond. It had the appearance from a distance of a man on the ground.

As they neared the fallen man, it became apparent that he was wearing the brown uniform of one of the Butcher's men. They could see that he was moving, but the gaping wound in the man's stomach ensured he would not be alive much longer.

Edmond and Anne dismounted near the crumpled figure, keeping a wary distance, while the others rode ahead slowly. The man's horse nervously stood nearby, shaken by what had recently happened. Anne moved to it. The horse started to back away. She caught a rein and halted its retreat. Her hand gently rubbed the horse's muzzle to calm the animal.

"Fools!" rasped the man on the ground in a faint, dry voice, drawing Anne's attention back to the dying soldier.

"Punishment for a thief and arsonist," said Edmond, responding, unmoved.

Perkins called from the crest of the low hill, anguish in his voice. "Sir, you'd better come up." Edmond and Anne ran up the hill.

As they reached the crest, they took in the horrific scene of a small but devastating fight. Several bodies were strewn about, some piled atop each other and none of them the massive size of the Butcher. In fact, every single body bore Lord Aylesbury's blue colors. All were Edmond's men.

"Dear God in heaven," mumbled Brother Mallory, as he caught sight of the massacre. Anne's knees caved in under her, and she slumped to the ground, turning her head away from the devastation. Never had she imagined, let alone witnessed, anything like this.

Even Edmond's balance started to give slightly. He turned to Boyles, and in a shaky voice, ordered him to scout the area and try to determine in which direction the killers were headed. He asked Mallory to administer last rites to the fallen.

As Edmond began to lower his head in silent prayer, he heard a faint groan from nearby. "See to it, Salgar," he ordered.

Salgar moved quickly to the site. There was a haphazard pile of bodies. A man lying against a dead horse seemed to be the source of the sound. Bending over the man, Salgar turned his head toward Edmond. "But, he's long dead, sir," he said, visibly shaken by the experience.

"Spirit of the dead?" speculated Perkins as Salgar began to walk back toward Edmond.

But the groaning continued. As the others looked on in horror, Edmond rushed to the body, suddenly realizing what was happening. He lifted the dead man's shoulder, nodded with new conviction, and turned his head back to Salgar. "Come help me. Someone's pinned underneath the dead man and he's still alive. *Hurry.*"

Respectfully, Salgar and Edmond shifted the dead man's body, revealing Dorsay stirring beneath.

"Edmond, boy," he said in a weak, raspy voice.

"Dorsay, old man!" said Edmond, obviously much relieved. He looked over at the monk. "How are you with healing, Brother Mallory?"

"I know a few things. His blood's from a r-ripping of the scalp. It appears to b-be very slight."

"I took a blow to the head," said Dorsay, wincing as Mallory examined the wound. "Argh. Don't waste it on me. See to the others!"

Obeying, Mallory stood up and walked among the other men, looking for signs of life.

"What happened?" asked Edmond, his voice laden with sadness and guilt.

Dorsay took a swig from Edmond's water skin, wishing it were spirits. He wiped his mouth with his sleeve, looked Edmond straight in the eye, then averted his gaze, as if repenting for failure. "I know we got one of them really good, and a few must be wounded."

"That's true," said Edmond. "One of them is on his way to his maker. But everyone else is gone. All of the men who were with you. In one day!"

Dorsay repositioned himself, wincing at the great pain.

"The Butcher. He cut us down like wheat. I have failed you in your quest, Captain."

"Not so. It is I who have failed as a captain. I should have been here with you."

"And you might have died under the devil's hand, as well. Now, help me up."

Using his shoulder as support for the wounded warrior, Edmond heaved Dorsay up gently.

"How is your leg?" the captain asked as they attempted a few steps.

"Could be broken, but I think I can still ride. Whatever it is, this leg has had it. It's useless now."

"Old man, at first I thought *you* had completely had it this time."

"Set me down by that stump and have them bring wood and kindling. I'll make a fire for camp. I must be useful for something."

Boyle, Salgar, and Perkins began to dig graves to hold the bodies, while Anne remained sitting at the crest of the hill, staring at the devastation through glazed eyes. She held the reins of several horses in her hands, including the one she had calmed when they arrived. No escape. No tricks. Her arms rested on her knees. Her head drooped slowly to rest on her arms and she remained there, alone with her thoughts of the day's events.

Just a few days past, I was wondering what life is like among the nobles. Now I have found out in the worst way. Will I ever get back to my family again? Will I ever be with my father on the sea again? Who will care for mother and little John? So many questions. So few answers.

Deep sadness wove into her thoughts. Tears flooded Anne's eyes, and she began to weep silently for herself, her family, and the men who lost their lives that day.

CHAPTER 15

Thursday Night, Close to Midnight
The Campsite Southwest of Wells

THE TONE WAS SOLEMN AND the air thick with smoke. Salgar, Anne, and Brother Mallory hunched around the campfire in silence. Mallory was doing his best to read a handwritten scroll by the light of the fire. The pack of texts was next to him on the ground. Anne was drawing in the sand with a stick.

A short distance away, by the horses, Perkins was out cold. He had drowned the day's despair in the ale he had emptied from his water skin into his belly.

Jerra Boyles appeared from the brush and dropped a load of dry twigs and branches just far enough away from the crackling fire to avoid catching them on fire.

"Where's the Cap?" he asked Salgar.

"Over by the graves with Dorsay."

Anne looked up. "They're deciding what to do about this quest now."

"An' payin' respects, I 'spect, too," said Salgar.

"So what is going to happen now . . . ?" Anne thought aloud, her voice trailing off.

"Not for us to worry about," Boyles came back.

"We can continue to the Sword, can't we?" she persisted.

"Well, we can't get to it anyway," Salgar said. "We've no idea where they've gone."

"To an island," said Mallory. "They've gone somewhere where there's an island in a lake."

"Aye and the mute's stopped stammering," noticed Boyles.

"Nervous habit," Mallory shrugged, as the others also realized that the stuttering had stopped.

"How do you know they've gone to an island?" asked Anne.

"What?" asked Mallory.

Anne repeated her question.

"Oh! Well, the Brothers' Burden stone says so."

"How do the stones work, anyway?" she asked.

"There are three parts to the journey," Mallory answered. "A stone for each part, I think. And at the end, the stones have to nest together. To be used together, somehow."

"So there's a third stone?"

"Yes, there is," Mallory nodded. "It's called the Lady's Blessing."

"Where are they going to get the third stone?"

"Well, the first two stones lead to the third stone. The Brothers' Burden, together with the King's Birthright, leads to the Lady's Blessing. It's on the island I've been speaking about. It's supposed to be guarded by the Lady of the Lake herself, if you believe in such spirits."

"Spirits?" asked Salgar, suddenly uncomfortable.

"Wait!" said Anne. "So that means the Butcher would need our stone, right?"

"Why, yes!" said Mallory. "Father Antony must have been keeping that part secret from the Butcher."

"So, we have an advantage after all," said Anne. "Do you have any idea where the island is? Off what coast? Near what town?"

"All I know is that it's an island in the middle of a lake," said Mallory sadly.

"That has to be enough," said Anne as she gathered some of the campfire cooking in a handkerchief and bolted from the camp toward the grave sites. In her wake, Mallory stood up to follow, yelling ahead to Anne.

"But you would need maps at the very least!" he called in exasperation.

Anne crested the hill just as the moon poked out from behind a cloud to reveal a landscape of freshly laid graves, each with an upright sword marking the land like a cross. Edmond was squatting next to one of the graves, his hand lightly touching the damp grass to his side. Dorsay stood near him, leaning upon a newly cut tree branch, which acted like a tall cane.

It was obvious they had been discussing the journey. A saddlebag overflowing with maps lay next to Edmond.

"All of these men lost," sighed Edmond.

"If you had been here, you probably would have been killed, too," said Dorsay, quietly. "The best thing is to go home and end this political rubbish."

"Do you really think it's rubbish, Dorsay?"

"In my opinion, the throne must be earned. Sword or not."

"Edmond?" Anne interrupted respectfully. Brother Mallory arrived a moment later. Standing just behind Anne, he was panting like an overheated dog.

"What is it, Anne?" Edmond asked kindly, noticing for the first time that she used his name instead of his rank to address him.

"First of all, you should eat," she said as she stretched both hands in front of her to offer the handkerchief laden with food. He took it and opened it at his feet, picking at the cooked meat with one hand.

"Thank you," he said, in an almost affectionate tone as he looked at her.

Dorsay limped away toward the campfire to get some food. His parting comment was, "She's right! Eat. I'm going to put this behind me, at any rate. Brother Mallory, would you help me down the hill?"

Dorsay fumbled his way down with the awkward walking staff poking the ground just ahead. Mallory dove under his arm to offer the warrior more stability and support. Just as the two were nearly out of sight, Dorsay called back, "Mourn them, but don't become one of them, Edmond, boy. Eat."

Edmond stared after his old friend and scratched his chin in thought. Then he turned toward Anne. "Something else?"

"We think we know where the Butcher's heading," she said, trying to contain her excitement.

"He's headed south, and we're going home."

"Why?"

"It's time. I don't have the means to defeat the Butcher."

"If you gain the Sword first, don't you win? The Butcher can't be king if he doesn't have the Sword, right?"

"He's far ahead of us and his group is stronger," he said, ignoring her question.

Anne's eyes darted to the leather bag with stained, rolled parchment maps sticking out of the opening. "You don't understand! Brother Mallory thinks the stones work together somehow, like a key. I think we're smarter, and they don't have the second stone. We do."

"I'm not going to end more lives for the sake of the Sword and the treasure, Anne."

"But, we're so close!"

"We actually have no idea how far or close we are."

"But we can figure it out, can't we?" persisted Anne as she snapped up the pouch holding the maps and bounded for the campsite.

"Anne, give them over," said Edmond, snatching after the pouch and missing it.

"I'm not ready to live in an England where the king is the man who tried to burn down that monastery. Are you?"

Frustrated, Edmond strode after Anne, refusing to run.

"Brother Mallory, help me find the map of the island," said Anne, as she entered the encampment, immediately dropping the maps to the ground near the fire.

Mallory dropped to his knees, shuffling through the parchments and attempting to identify each map. Together, they spread the maps out as each was unrolled.

Running out of space in front of her, Anne spotted Perkins asleep next to her. She shrugged and laid an open map over his inert shape. Perkins continued his drunken snoring, slightly muffled by the map atop him, but otherwise unbothered.

Boyles was poised over Anne's shoulder, applying his experience as a scout to the study of the maps. At Boyles's silent urging, even Salgar grabbed one of the parchments, which turned out to also be a map. He stretched it out in front of him.

Anne looked up to see Edmond arriving on the scene. She could tell from his expression that the sight of nearly every member of the camp leaning over a map was less than pleasing to him.

Edmond loudly cleared his throat to gain their attention.

Salgar looked up from studying a map. "Sir, I think they might have something here."

Anne looked at Salgar in a new light.

"Look, Captain," said Mallory, pointing to one of the maps. "Here is the area around the order's monastery." He pointed to a symbol of a cross. Mallory continued to unfurl one map after another, placing each around and overlapping other maps, fitting together one large mapped area.

"We've got most of England here, right?" asked Anne.

"Give or take a land. We're missing an awful large part of the north," said Mallory, unsettled by Edmond looking over his shoulder.

"So help me here, everyone," said Anne, exhibiting effortless leadership of the group. "How many lakes have islands or are big enough for islands?"

Each looked over the map area directly in front of them, reporting back to Anne, one at a time.

"There are three to the east," said Boyles.

"I've got two possible sites by the southern coastline," reported Mallory.

"I've got one possibility to the northeast," came Salgar.

"You've got the western section, miss," said Mallory.

"It's Anne, thanks. Yes, there's one right here. It's near a town. What does that word say, Edmond?"

"Glastonbury," said Edmond. "That's seven possibilities. How can we cover most of England before the Butcher gets there?"

Dorsay hobbled into the firelight after checking the horses. He looked over the scene. "What is this?"

"They think they know where the Butcher is," said Edmond.

"Think?" Anne turned to them. "Look, we're narrowing it down."

Dorsay shook his head. "We should forget all of it and pack up."

"I think we know which one, sir," said Salgar.

Edmond looked at his soldier. "What did you say?"

The whole camp turned to listen to Salgar. "Well, the Butcher headed southwest from the battle area."

Boyles nodded. "If he thought he killed the whole battalion, he probably wasn't feigning it either."

"So we *do* know where he went," said the captain.

A disgusted look crept across Dorsay's face. "Whatever you might be thinking, Edmond, we should *not* go. We haven't the force."

Edmond disagreed with his friend. "But they're right! We might be able to beat them there."

"Be realistic," said Dorsay. "I'm wounded. We've no fresh horses to continue pursuit. We can't fight them."

Anne held up the inscribed stone. "They still don't have the monk's stone. And look at the mark on this other map!"

"Where is that?" Edmond asked.

"Glastonbury!" said Mallory and, for emphasis, Anne slammed her hand on the lake marked on the map.

"Please! Stop!" the map seemed to shout, mysteriously moving of its own accord. The group pulled back as the parchment slipped aside, revealing Perkins with his hand over one eye. He looked back and forth at the faces staring at him. "Uh, oh. Did I miss the night watch?"

The tension of the past several minutes fell away. Everyone stared at Perkins, smiles slowly growing on the faces of all except Dorsay. Salgar and Boyles tried hard to hold their laughter.

Perkins eyed everyone for seconds more, then rolled over to go back to sleep. "Bloody staring at a bloody man trying to get his bloody sleep," he muttered.

The captain turned away from Perkins. "Well then, Salgar, prepare everything for a long ride in the morning."

Edmond turned and half marched to his small tent, posted a short distance from the campfire. Dorsay hobbled after him.

"This is ridiculous," Dorsay said again behind him.

"Stop it, Dorsay. Rest. That's an order," said Edmond, irritation creeping into his voice. He added, almost sarcastically, "You can stay behind, if you wish."

"I'm warning you, Edmond, this will all go very badly if we meet the Butcher again in battle." Dorsay gestured back toward the fire. "Do you want to risk *their* lives, too?"

"What's gotten into you?" asked Edmond, becoming more exasperated with Dorsay by the minute.

"What's gotten into *you*, Edmond? Just because of some girl you take a fancy to—"

Edmond stopped in his tracks and turned on Dorsay. "You are out of line! You may be my elder, but you are not my superior! Get ready for the morning or go to bed, soldier!"

Edmond stooped to enter his small tent.

Through clenched teeth, Dorsay began, "Yes. You are the—"

"*Captain*." interrupted Edmond, finishing the sentence. "*Your* captain." And, with that, Edmond drew closed the flap.

CHAPTER 16

Friday, Midafternoon
A Forest Track Northeast of Glastonbury

THE SCOUT KNEELED OVER A set of tracks. Among them, one set of hoofprints stood out, large and deep. It was the prints of the Butcher's massive warhorse, Boyles had no doubt of that. He looked up at Edmond on his horse, a cloudy sky behind him. Edmond nodded approval. Boyles mounted up and the company moved on.

A few hours later, they stopped at a small pond on the edge of a rock quarry to water the horses.

The going was slow as they led their horses on foot over the excavations, which continued for about half a mile.

The path was treacherous, and at one point Anne slipped on a smooth rock face. Edmond offered her his hand with a smile. She stared at it, then at him, before gracefully taking hold. He helped her up the rock face as she returned his smile. Nearby, Dorsay looked irritated at the sight of the two.

It was nearly twilight when the captain, on horseback again, rolled up a map and looked to Anne and Mallory, who were flanking him on horseback.

Any time now, Edmond thought.

"To think that we are so close to the lost Sword," said Mallory.

Anne looked across Edmond at the monk. "Do *you* also want to conquer the world, Brother Mallory?"

"Actually," Mallory replied, "it is the sheath that interests me more."

"The sheath? Why?" Edmond asked.

"It is written that Arthur once asked his counselor, Merlin, what he thought more valuable. Merlin answered that it was the sheath he should protect at all costs, not the Sword. When Arthur asked the reason, Merlin said, 'The sheath protects, while the Sword only serves to destroy others.' I think that says much."

"Peace is more desirable than war," commented Anne.

Mallory tilted his head, appraising Anne. "Yes. Exactly."

Edmond, too, glanced at her with a certain respect.

They rode over the crest of a small hill. "We have arrived," said Edmond, looking down.

Below them, the bustling town of Glastonbury glowed in the blue twilight of the evening. Blacksmiths' smoke hung in the air, and hawkers in the marketplace could be heard from a distance over the din of people and horses. The group could also see the large lake behind the town. Next to the lake, on a hill, was the steeple of an abbey. Several small hills atop islands were visible in the distance.

The sun had set when the party rode into the town. They brought their horses to a stop in front of an inn with a sign identifying it as The Green Elf. After rooms were arranged with the innkeeper, followed by a dinner served up by the innkeeper's wife, Edmond, Anne, and Mallory gathered in a private room at the back of the inn.

Anne noted that the room was tidy and the furniture simple. The only window in the room had been shuttered, and several lamps made of cows' horns cast light over a table that seemed somehow too large for the room.

There they studied the parchment maps and the stone, trying to piece together the puzzle.

"We still need a starting point on the island, where the stone leaves off," said Mallory.

"Which," replied Edmond, "is part of the reason Father Antony is the next stop on our list."

Mallory looked up from the map. "Do you think he is still . . . "

"Alive?" Edmond completed the question. "They need him to get to the end. If they have not found it yet, then he is very much alive."

Dorsay entered the room and shut the door quietly behind him.

"There is no mention of them in the town, Captain," reported Dorsay.

Five minutes later, Boyles entered. "I have spotted them. Their camp is on the western shore of the largest lake. There are several boats; one on the center island is empty, and there is another identical one on the western island."

"Why would they search on more than one island?" asked Anne.

"Because they don't know *which* island it's on," surmised Edmond.

"Maybe someone found it first," said Dorsay.

"The Sword of all swords?" asked Edmond. "Seems like we would have known."

"Then that's good news," said Anne. "We still have a chance of finding it first."

Edmond nodded. "All the more reason to retrieve the other stone and Father Antony *tonight*."

CHAPTER 17

Late Friday Evening
An Encampment on the West Shore of the Lake

MOONLIGHT SHIMMERING ON THE LAKE water silhouetted three boats tied to a post on the shore. Lurch, the Butcher's second-in-command, was sitting on the ground in front of a similar post, whittling at a piece of wood and occasionally glancing at the islands.

Suddenly he stopped his whittling and turned his ear toward one of the islands close to shore. He thought he heard a splash in the water.

Around the campfire at Lurch's back, six men lay on their thin pallets, snoring loudly. Lurch looked at the men, then back at the water.

Satisfied it was a snore he had heard, Lurch returned to his whittling.

Two small series of splashes again came from the direction of the island. This time Lurch's head jerked up.

Another splash.

Lurch carefully set his woodworking project down and slinked away from the encampment in the direction of the sound. He placed his whittling knife flat between his teeth, giving him the appearance of a grim pirate.

At one edge of the camp, a line of horses was slumbering. At the end of the horse line, tied like the horses beside him, Father Antony leaned against the tree to which he was secured by a rope around his portly middle. His eyelids slowly fluttered open and closed as he unsuccessfully attempted to grasp a wisp of sleep here and there despite his uncomfortable position.

Out of the darkness, a hand slowly rested on the holy man's shoulder. Startled, he turned abruptly as another hand clasped his mouth to stifle a frightened scream. Father Antony could now see the face of Dorsay, who quickly raised one finger to his lips as he eased the other hand away from the monk's mouth.

Still scared, Father Antony mouthed, "Who are you?"

Another apparition, Edmond, replied with a whisper, "Brother Mallory sent us."

Smiling widely now, and mouthing a prayer of thanks heavenward, Father Antony offered his bound wrists for Dorsay to cut him free.

At another point on the lakeshore stood a tall, wide tent. Spears were stuck in the ground like inanimate sentries before the entrance.

The interior seemed completely filled by the Butcher's massive frame. Even sleeping, the man wore his dented and heavy armor.

In one corner of the tent, a small knife blade suddenly and silently jutted through the cloth wall, carefully slicing a small line downward, then sideways, then upward, creating a flap door.

Without the slightest sound, Boyles inched his way into the tent. On the other side of the Butcher's body, he could barely make out, by the moonlight filtering in through the flap he had cut, a row of bags and the red box with the golden dragon on it, out in the open.

To get the box, he would have to grab it by stretching over the tent's occupant. Boyles rolled his eyes. *Why couldn't I have entered on the other side of this brute*?

Carefully reaching over the massive frame, which heaved with each slow, windy breath, Boyles reached the box and lifted it with ease, slowly elevating it over the Butcher toward himself.

Midway through the exercise, the Butcher snorted as if he had swallowed an insect. Thinking the huge man was about to move or turn over, Boyles froze, listening for the giant's next move and worrying that the Butcher might awaken suddenly. But that didn't happen. The Butcher went quiet again, as if slipping into a deeper sleep.

Satisfied that he could complete his task, Boyles pulled the box silently over the giant.

Once he had it on his side of the tent, he smiled with relief and slid the box to the outside. Boyles then carefully slithered out of the tent like a snake.

Anne sat on the edge of a hill, which masked her, and the horses whose reins she held, from those looking up from below on the other side. Out of the corner of her eye, she saw a large frame emerging from around a bend. Startled to the edge of screaming, she caught herself when she recognized the figure.

"God, you scared me."

"Calm," said Dorsay, limping against his walking stick. "All's well."

Edmond, heaving Father Antony's weight on his shoulder, rounded the bend. Seeing them, Anne pulled out a water skin from the nearest horse's saddlebag and offered a drink to the monk. He smiled weakly, taking a long pull of the liquid.

"Where's Boyles?" Edmond asked.

"Don't know," replied Anne.

Edmond helped the monk onto a horse just as Boyles rounded the corner.

"*Voila*!" Boyles declared, holding up the red box in his hands.

"Excellent," Edmond said. "Now, let's get out of here."

They mounted their horses and cantered toward the town.

Boyles moved his horse to Edmond's side. "Sir."

"Good job with that, Boyles."

"It was easy, sir. Almost a little too easy for my liking."

Anne, on Edmond's other side, thought the captain looked a bit more thoughtful than she would have expected after two major successes that evening.

CHAPTER 18

Friday – Just Before Midnight
The Inn at Glastonbury

IN THE BACK ROOM OF the inn, the red gilded box was set gently on a table covered with several of the maps they were studying at the encampment.

Brother Mallory slowly opened the box and revealed the stone disk within. As he lifted it from the box, Anne noticed that, like the Brothers' Burden, this was an intricately carved disk with a hole in the middle. It was larger than the Brothers' Burden, and it suddenly occurred to her that the Burden stone could exactly fit into the larger disk's hole.

Mallory held the Burden stone in front of the hole for all to see the match. "I give you the King's Birthright," he announced in a quiet voice.

Then he slowly lowered the Brothers' Burden into the center of the King's Birthright. "Amazing. No doubt they were crafted by the same maker. I have never seen the like of this work."

"They're beautiful," said Anne.

But Edmond was all business. "So how do they lead to the Sword?"

"They don't," came Father Antony's raspy voice from across the room.

All eyes shifted to the elderly monk hunched weakly in a chair in the corner.

Edmond frowned. "I don't understand."

"It is quite simple," said Father Antony. "These two stones together lead to the third stone."

"The Lady's Blessing?" asked Anne.

"Yes, my child," Father Antony replied. "And the three of them all together lead to the Sword." Father Antony gradually lifted his large frame from the chair and slowly walked to them, using the edge of the table for support as he studied the married stones. He nodded with pride at Mallory, and then, using an index finger, he slowly traced words carved along the thin edge of the larger stone.

"See this here?" he asked, looking from face to face around the table to be quite certain he had everybody's full attention.

"Well, the first part here are the directions to where we are now," he continued. His finger jumped to the map portion on the face of the stones. "To the north of this and the west of that. But the important bit comes here."

Now Father Antony's finger slowly moved to the center of the face of the larger disk, tracing words that wound around from stone to stone. Only when the two stones nestled together were the words complete and readable.

Father Antony read the inscription aloud: "*In the center, the Lady will show them the way to the test, and they will meet under the blessings of Avalon.*"

"Avalon is an island?" ventured Edmond.

"That's correct," said the monk. "However, I know that the Butcher has combed over each of the three small islands, and he has found nothing. Right? There should be a marker, or stones, something to mark where the pagan worship site of Avalon was located. Just as it says here on the stone *in the center* and *under Avalon*."

"Maybe the Butcher missed something?" Edmond suggested.

"No, he didn't. I saw it myself," said Father Antony. "They took me with them as they searched. There was nothing in the center of those three islands. Nothing but bushes and trees."

Anne had been listening quietly. "What does it mean when it says *the Lady will show them*?" she asked the monk.

"Probably a marker," said Mallory. "A small shrine or a statue perhaps."

"Begging your pardon, sir," Boyles looked up at Edmond. "If we don't know how to get this stone, we should be getting on. When the Butcher finds out his big pebble's missing, no inn will protect us."

"But we need just a little time to sort it out," said Anne.

"I will give you two hours, then," said Edmond. "I will be in my quarters. Advise me if you discover any further clues." He turned and left the room.

Immediately, Brother Mallory and Father Antony began to study the maps and the stones. At one point, Mallory separated the nestled stones and lifted the larger disk over one of the maps. As he circled over the map they both peered through the large center hole of the King's Birthright, trying to make sense of what lay below. Father Antony, growing very tired, sipped water from a wooden cup on the table before suggesting they rest a bit.

Anne had been watching over Mallory's shoulder for a while. When the two holy men took their break for some rest, Anne took up the cause. She leaned over the maps, trying to no avail to make some sense of it all.

A little before two o'clock in the morning, Edmond returned. He glanced at the figures slumped in chairs around the room, sleeping. Then his eyes turned to the table where Anne, the only one awake, was still poised over the maps, licking her lips and sliding the smaller of the two stone disks around between her hand and the table, making a grating noise.

"Stop it, for God's sake," said Edmond.

She immediately realized what was irking him and stopped pushing the stone around the table. The irritating noise stopped. He came closer.

Thinking better of his reaction, he apologized. "No, I'm sorry, Anne. I'm very tired. There was no excuse for snapping at you."

"It's all right," she replied, gesturing to the sleeping monks. "We're all so tired. But I feel as though I'm so close to figuring this out. I thought maybe the stones could be used together with the maps."

"I didn't think of that," he said.

"Well, probably because you're smarter than me. The map would have had to have been made at the same time as the stones."

Edmond leaned over her shoulder, pointing tentatively at one of the maps and positioning one of the stones so the inscription could be read. "I thought maybe the inscriptions had the location in code. But they only point to an island on a lake and—"

Anne turned her head away from the map and, unaware of Edmond's closeness, now found her face startlingly close to his. Neither moved away from the other.

"—and I'm sure we're not finished here yet." She completed his sentence.

"How do you do that?" he asked.

"Do what?"

"You keep going forward, even when everything looks its blackest?"

"I guess I'm too stubborn to know when I've lost," she said quietly.

With nobody watching them at the moment, station and position seemed to melt away, and they both edged a little closer.

Her eyes fixed intently on Edmond, Anne's movement caused her hand to brush a wooden cup on the table, knocking it over and spilling water on the maps. The cup rolled to the floor with a clatter. The noise stirred the slumbering holy men.

Immediately the moment was broken. Anne turned back to the table instantly, leaving Edmond slightly biting his lower lip.

"The maps!" Anne exclaimed, trying to wipe the water away with the sleeve of her shirt.

"No! Stop!" Edmond said. "The ink will run. They'll be useless." He handed her a nearby cloth napkin and began collecting the maps strewn around the area.

There was a slight knock on the door.

"Come," said Edmond.

Dorsay entered, his shoes wet with mud.

"You said you wanted a reminder at two o'clock, Captain," said Dorsay.

"Yes," replied Edmond, his eyes full of disappointment as he surveyed the wet maps strewn across the table. "You were right, Dorsay. Pack everything up for home."

Anne, however, could not tear her eyes from the wet maps still directly in front of her. She focused on a map that depicted the lake closest to Glastonbury and its three islands. The cup's spilled water, seeping through the parchment, had already made a stain on the map, worsened by Anne's attempts to wipe it off with her sleeve. She watched as the stain slowly filled the area of the lake, and more interestingly, seeped around the monastery's hill, while the depiction of the monastery remained dry.

"Wait!" she said, eyes transfixed on the map. "Father Antony, my grandmother used to speak of how our house was once a little farther from the ocean. It was her joke that the ocean would one day fish for the fishermen. Is it possible that in eight hundred years, the land could have changed enough to cause the lake's shore to change?"

"I don't know," said Father Antony, thoughtfully. "I suppose it is possible. The lake might dry up and recede. Or be used up."

Edmond and the monks quickly gathered again around the maps. Anne pointed out the stain surrounding the hill drawn on the map.

"It makes sense," she said. "There are abbey ruins at the center of a hill, right at the edge of the lake. And it's the tallest hill! Maybe it was once surrounded by water. Maybe that hill was once an island?"

"It is possible," said Father Antony. "*All* things are possible in God."

"Only one way to find out," said Edmond. "Men—" Anne caught his eye and he corrected. "Uh—people—let's have a look."

He turned and passed the others on his way to the door. *Is there a smile on her face*? he thought as he passed Anne.

CHAPTER 19

Saturday – Three O'Clock in the Morning
Atop Glastonbury Tor

In the near-darkness of the waning moon, the company arrived at the top of the steep hill known as Glastonbury Tor. Anne noticed the group's uneasy glances toward the other end of the lake where the rogues would be slumbering in their peaceful camp.

As they proceeded along the top of the hill, they came to the remains of a once-thriving abbey. All they could see at first was a wall and the entry arch, which framed a courtyard.

"We must look for anything out of place within the ruins," Father Antony said quietly.

"Like what?" Anne asked quietly.

"Something that will harken back to the past when the pagan gods were revered."

The group scanned everything: the arches, the columns, even rocks haphazardly strewn about in the courtyard.

Salgar and Perkins were trying their best to read the inscriptions on the few gravestones beyond the courtyard.

Edmond was about to ride through what would have been the entrance when he heard a cough from Father Antony. Looking toward the origin of the noise, he noticed suddenly that everyone but him had dismounted out of respect for the hallowed grounds. Blushing, the captain dismounted, tying his horse to a leaning column.

The company walked slowly further into the courtyard, which occupied the exact center of the hill.

"We can light torches now," Edmond said. "But keep them low to the ground."

Salgar immediately took a small piece of wood and tinder from his saddlebag and knelt down to set a fire by friction. Within a few minutes, his small fire was used for the lighting of several small torches.

The courtyard was covered in flat, uneven stones overgrown by plant life. In its center was an iconic statue clothed like the Virgin Mary. Edmond dropped his pack beside the statue and lit his small torch from Salgar's ground fire.

The torch, rich with oil, burned brightly within seconds, shedding orange light on the carvings adorning the base of the statue. The pedestal itself was almost as tall as Edmond.

Something caught his eye. He turned toward the closest monk. "Father Antony," he inquired, "since when is the Virgin Mother surrounded by . . . fish?"

As the rest of the group approached, Edmond lifted his torch from the weathered carvings of fish around the pedestal upward to near the statue's face.

Her serene facial expression and welcoming appearance made it easy to understand how she might have been mistaken for the Mother of Christ. Around the neck of the figure, a necklace ended with a crucifix, which rested on her heart.

But the rest of the figure hardly seemed Christian in design.

Anne was amazed at how the statue's hair seemed to sway realistically in the wind beneath its hood.

The crucifix moved slightly as Mallory brushed his fingertips over its surface. His eyes on the movement of the crucifix, Father Antony mumbled softly, "Sometimes it is necessary to replace other gods with our own."

"Disguising the truth to bring the truth," said Edmond.

Anne was fascinated. "Did it not say on the stone, *The Lady will show the way*?"

She gazed at the statue as she lifted her torch slowly. In its pose, one hand of the figure rested gracefully on her heart, her head looking down upon her audience, much as if she were the Virgin Mother.

Anne shifted her torch in the direction of the other hand. It held what looked like a weighing scale. At the center of the scale's tray was a thick, round pin, carved to look like a short stack of river stones.

Edmond and Anne exchanged looks.

"So, putting it all together will show us how to find the third stone disk?" Edmond asked, glancing at Mallory.

"It makes sense," replied Mallory.

"It's certainly worth a try, isn't it?" urged Anne.

Edmond opened his saddlebag and removed the gilded-dragon box. Opening it, he revealed the two stones tightly nestled together. Edmond laid the larger of the two on the tray of the scale.

Nothing happened.

Anne looked anxiously at Edmond. "Nest the smaller stone within it."

As Edmond followed Anne's directions, it was quickly apparent that all the pieces were carved to fit. The smaller stone disk snapped onto the carved pin on the scale tray, and the larger stone disk embraced the smaller one.

"Sunrise is almost here," said Dorsay. "If this doesn't work . . ."

Suddenly the pin shaped like a stack of river stones sank into the tray about an inch and the party heard a sound like two massive stones grinding together.

But nothing in the statue changed.

"Well," Edmond asked, "did anything just happen?"

Both he and Anne looked over the front of the statue carefully. *Nothing appears to have changed*, thought

Anne. She looked at Edmond as if to say, "what now?" In response, he began to inch around to the figure's back.

There they saw it.

At the rear, the entire wall of the pedestal was missing, exposing an opening to what looked like a passage.

Anne shone her torch into the passage. Except for spider webs, only the floor of the tunnel caught the torchlight.

"Truly astounding," said Mallory.

"Nervous already?" Anne asked, offering a tension-breaking smile. "We're not even there yet."

Edmond moved to the front of the statue and removed the Burden and Birthright stones cautiously, one by one. He placed them in a pouch affixed to the belt of his uniform. Wondering whether the pedestal door would close again, Edmond noted that the stack of river stones was still set within the scale tray.

The pedestal door remained open.

"Dorsay, Brother Mallory and Father Antony, come with me. Anne, you remain here," Edmond ordered.

One by one, they entered the passage beneath the statue, walking downward into the darkness beyond the entrance.

"Surely you must be joking!" an indignant Anne called after Edmond. "Don't think for a minute that you're not taking me!"

"You have no idea what might be down there," said Edmond, turning to face her from just inside the entrance.

"And *you* do?" asked Anne. "I'm going."

"No, you are not. This time I'm putting my foot down. You are staying here for your own good. Salgar!"

Salgar came up behind Anne and grabbed hold of her arms.

Edmond continued, turning back to follow the tunnel. "Boyle, keep watch. Salgar and Perkins, watch her. *Protect* her," he called back to them. Edmond's voice sounded farther away now, almost muffled, as it wafted from the tunnel.

"How can you do this after all I've done to help?" Anne complained into the darkness.

"Worry not," Edmond's voice echoed along the tunnel. "You'll still get a share of the treasure."

"I really don't care about the gold . . . " protested Anne, futilely straining to free herself from Salgar's grip. Then, in a whisper that Edmond would not hear from within, she added, "I care about *you*."

Hearing this, Salgar loosened his grip, but only enough to get a rope around Anne's arms.

CHAPTER 20

Saturday – Dawn

THE TORCH SEEMED TO ONLY shed light a few feet in any direction as they descended into the earth.

Mallory's mouth was twisted in a queasy expression. Dorsay, seeing this, gave him a good slap on the back. "Ah, it's not hell yet, monk."

This did not cheer Mallory in the slightest, and the group continued forward slowly, Dorsay painfully grunting at every step.

"Looks like there's an opening up ahead," said Edmond.

Directly above the tunnel, dawn replaced the night as the sky began to brighten with the sun breaking over the eastern horizon.

Anne's hands were tied together in front of her by a rope around her wrists. Her ankles were bound with a ridiculous overabundance of rope. Next to her, Perkins was on one knee tying the last of the knots.

"We do like you, Miss. But we'z got orders to do this y'know."

Perkins stood and walked over to another fire they had started building to keep them warm near the opening in the statue's pedestal.

Anne amused herself by tracing with her hands the intricately carved fish designs on the large pedestal.

One design almost immediately caught her attention. It was larger than any of the other fish and amazingly detailed such that the weathering seemed minimal.

It bore a striking resemblance to a pike. A sea monster by the size of it, she thought, staring at the fish's large mouth, open to bare long, narrow teeth.

With her forefinger, she traced one of the fangs, which actually jutted out from the pedestal.

Hissing, she drew her finger back and looked at a small prick on the tip of her finger. She lifted her arms, bindings and all, and began to suck on her bleeding fingertip.

Then an idea struck her. Gathering herself as close as possible to the statue, she began to rub the ropes that were around her wrists in a back and forth sawing motion against the same sharp stone tooth of the pike that had cut her finger.

A few minutes later, she had nearly severed the rope when she heard footsteps and stopped abruptly.

She heard an exchange on the other side of the pedestal.

"Where's the other two horses?" Salgar asked Perkins.

"Wot?"

"There were two more horses tied to the pillar over yonder."

"Dunno. Maybe they moved?"

Salgar walked off, muttering to himself. "Now I'm a stable boy as well as a woman's jailer. I never get to be the bloody soldier, do I?"

Anne resumed her attempt to cut the ropes against the stone tooth, and a few minutes later was rewarded as she looped the nearly severed rope over the large tooth and jerked hard. The rope split in two. She unraveled the loops binding her wrists, and was soon untying the knots in the rope binding her ankles.

Quietly, she rose to a crouch and peered around the statue base. She could see Perkins's back, a blanket draped over his shoulders as he attempted to light the fire.

Sensing the moment, she turned away, and keeping the pedestal between them for cover, made a quiet escape down the hill.

About fifty yards down, she heard horses' hooves. Fearing Salgar, she pressed her frame as best she could against a rocky outcropping.

Expecting to see the large frame of Salgar, she caught her breath at her first glimpse of the pursuer.

It wasn't Salgar, and it wasn't even a single horseman, but four.

All of them were henchmen of the Butcher.

Below ground, Edmond passed through the opening to a cavern, holding his torch in front of him to cast light as far ahead as possible. As he stood up from the crouching position required to navigate the last part of the tunnel, Edmond gazed up at the large cavern's high ceiling. Bits of light danced across it, reflections of the torchlight off the rippling surface of the water below.

Water? Thought Edmond, who was immediately distracted by the comments of Father Antony.

"I'm not sure how much more stooping my poor back can take," complained the priest.

"Well, at least we're here," Edmond said.

"Wherever here is," commented Dorsay.

"Oh my," said Mallory, awe in his voice. "It's the Lady's Chamber."

"Complete with torches," said Edmond seeing a shell-like sconce in the wall nearby. Inspecting more closely, his torch accidentally touched the sconce, which unexpectedly caught fire.

Suddenly, a blue flame traveled along a small, narrow trench leading out of the sconce and around the wall, following a trail of fragrant oil in the groove. The flame, in turn, lit other torches as it rushed forward in a ring around the chamber.

The light of the several torches now illuminated an immense space. Edmond and his followers were standing on a small platform at the edge of an underground lake. In the very center of the lake was a statue, and beyond that, another platform.

Edmond saw the ceiling and walls of the room were covered with paintings of surprising color and clarity, depicting the story of King Arthur. Even in the blue light, the dragon on Arthur's shield was as red as the blood in another scene, which depicted Arthur's death following the battle against his son, Mordred.

"How inventive," said Brother Mallory, sniffing at the fragrant substance around the edge of one sconce. The light from the torches seemed to grow brighter as their eyes adjusted. Now they could clearly see the statue of a woman on an islet at the center of the underground lake.

The Lady of the Lake.

Edmond studied the statue. Something about the face of the woman depicted caught his attention. Maybe it was the eyes? The shape of the nose and mouth? What could it be? And then it struck him. The face of the woman of the statue was virtually identical to Anne's. It was as if the Lady of the Lake were Anne du Lac's identical twin.

As quickly as the thought came to him, Edmond dismissed it to return his attention to the matter at hand. He looked again at the whole statue. Sitting gracefully on a rock, the Lady's left hand almost touched the surface of the pool. Just beneath the hand, the water churned, as though it were boiling.

"It must be a spring," Father Antony said. "That would explain why this lake is not dust. A spring is probably the source of the water for this pool." He turned slowly to take in the scenic grandeur of the cavern.

Brother Mallory, more scholar than theologian, examined the details rather than the scenery surrounding them. Dorsay wore an impassive expression, leaning against the wall to ease the apparent pain in his leg, like a soldier saving his energy for the task at hand.

Edmond's eyes continued to scan the details of the scene before him. Then he spotted it. His voice broke the silence. "I think we just found the third stone."

Everyone turned toward the statue. The Lady of the Lake's eyes were fixed on the churning water below. In her right hand, resting on her lap, lay a disk-shaped jewel, about the size of a man's eye.

"That stone in her hand must be the Lady's Blessing," said Mallory, his voice a reverent whisper.

Wrapped around the base of the statue was the rendering of an enormous fish. Its body was huge for a pike, resembling a marlin or large shark. The mouth was open, and from it, sculpted fangs jutted with startling length.

Edmond looked into the depths adjacent to the entry platform. Below, he spotted something swimming—something dark and massive.

"Did you see that?" he asked, still staring at the pool.

"Yes," said a voice right behind him, eyes fixed upon the jewel in the Lady's hand. "It will be perfect for Lambert's crown, don't you think, Edmond?"

Startled, Edmond suddenly felt the cold steel of a sword pressing against the back of his neck.

Dorsay's sword.

Edmond barely had room to turn, and when he did, he saw Dorsay, quite nimble, his leg easily supporting his weight.

"You're a fast healer," said Edmond, sarcastically.

"I did warn you, Edmond. I really did. I told you to turn back, and gave you every blasted chance."

Edmond's expression turned from shock to comprehension. "How much is Lambert giving you, Dorsay?"

"I offered him a dukedom," came a gruff sounding voice, as a large figure stepped from the shadows into the torchlight.

All eyes turned to see the Butcher, whose men easily restrained Mallory and Father Antony.

"I thought it was a fair offer," said the Butcher, "But all he wants is a general's post and some funds."

CHAPTER 21

Saturday – Early Morning
The Abbey Ruins

A LITTLE OVER A HUNDRED feet directly above the Butcher, the morning was now bathed in brilliant hues and colors, making it much easier for Anne to see into the ruins when she arrived back at the top of the hill.

Oh, wonderful! she thought bitterly as she spied Perkins, Salgar, and Boyle sitting with their backs to the pedestal beneath the statue of the Lady in the courtyard. All were gagged and bound.

A seedy man with the appearance of a famine-thin beggar was nearby. Another two henchmen sat guarding the entrance to the tunnel, their backs to the prisoners. One of them, covered head to toe in studded armor over his brown tunic, was fumbling in his saddlebag. The other, looking swollen in too-tight clothing, was impatiently dry washing his hands in a futile attempt to dispel the morning chill.

"Why'ent we killed 'em yet?" the armored brute asked.

"I don't want to carry them sacks of gold on me back, do you?" answered the fat one.

"Right," remarked the man in armor. "Let 'em do their work and then carve holes in 'em." The two brutes shared a rough laugh.

Meanwhile, the thin beggar was bent over Perkins, sifting through every pocket, every fold in the soldier's garments. He discovered Perkins's water skin and opened it, lifting the now-empty container to his lips. Disappointed, he threw it to one side.

"Eh, Hunder," said the man in armor. "What are you doin' pokin' about? Com'n get your food."

Anne crawled along the ground of the abandoned monastery toward the statue using her elbows.

She saw the man the guards had called Hunder squat like a frog by the campfire where the other henchmen were sitting. He sniffed at the offering. "No time for eating. Food's worth nothing. *Nothing*," he repeated.

Like a ferret, Hunder moved swiftly back to the prisoners, using his knife like a hand to look everywhere.

"Eh," said the man in armor. "Suit yourself then. I'll eat yer food."

Like a scorpion's tail striking, the fat one snatched at the tack and salted pork, saying, "No, you bloody fool. It's my turn for Hunder's rations."

The armored one snatched the food back, his voice rising. "You've gone blimey if you think you're cheatin' me out of this."

Taking advantage of the argument, Anne hurled a rock, which landed close by the gnome-like Hunder, but garnered no response. Hunder continued to explore for booty and mumble to himself.

" . . . Eh? Nothin'. Nothin' at all."

A second rock hit the statue. The arguing guards remained oblivious; however, this time Hunder immediately stood tall, looking around and even sniffing the air.

With his head turned the other way, Anne threw a third rock, this time into the open graveyard, where it clattered on the rock and granite.

"What? Ghosts?" Hunder mumbled. Intrigued, he started to walk toward the ruins, sniffing at rocks and lichen.

Anne threw a series of rocks that landed further and further away down the hillside, each one drawing Hunder down the hill away from the camp and her.

The two henchmen were still playing tug of war over the meat as Hunder passed them and walked out of sight, apparently going down toward the lake, following the noises made by Anne's rocks.

Anne began to slowly inch toward the campsite again. Suddenly, she was pulled to the ground by sweaty, grimy hands that reached from out of nowhere to cover her mouth.

"Thought you could fool Hunder, seeee . . . hmm?"

Anne squirmed, but despite Hunder's skeletal limbs, she was held fast by the beggar who now squatted atop her.

He slowly released the grip of the hand covering her mouth, whispering, "Girl don't want to scream. The guards are much worse than Hunder." He began to search her garments. "Where will Hunder find gold?"

Collin's clothes were tight over Anne's hips, making Hunder's one-handed search difficult, requiring him to struggle as he attempted to enter the trouser pockets.

"Women always hide their gold," he said. "Where is it?"

The advantage wasn't lost on Anne and she began to spin just enough to let gravity carry her fitfully down the hill. Hunder was forced to roll with her, his hand now pinned in her pocket.

Down the steep incline of the hill they both tumbled to the sounds of Hunder's bones crunching and his screeching with every bounce—until his head struck a large boulder and he went silent and limp.

Meanwhile, atop the Tor, the two remaining rogues were still struggling for Hunder's food over what was once the campfire. The armored henchman's face was now covered in soot from the dead fire. Each had a knife to the other's throat.

"Did you hear that?" asked the armored one.

"No one falls for that bit anymore," replied the fat rogue.

"No, wait, I'm serious!" said the man in armor. "I hear Hunder screeching!" He pulled his knife away from his attacking comrade and stood up quickly, distancing himself from the other. Placing his hand on the hilt of his sword, he turned and pulled off in the direction of the scream.

"Stay here," he called back to the fat one. "Touch the meat and I will have you for dinner myself, I will!"

The fat rogue sat up, brushing ashes from his shoulders. He glanced at the prisoners. Perkins, Salgar and Boyles were thoroughly tied up and gagged.

"An' don' you run away with yers. Scared stiff ye' were," the fat rogue told the restrained prisoners. He took a place atop a large stone and began rummaging through the armored one's bags for the meat, his back once again to the prisoners.

Anne emerged quietly over the crest of the hill on the other side of the abbey, dirty, torn, and a little bloody, but still very much intact. In her right hand she carried her latest prize, the long rusty knife Hunder had been using earlier.

Quietly, she sliced the bindings around Perkins's hand and mouth. He threw her a brief look of gratitude, whispering, "Oh, so help me, if we ever get through this mess, I'll never drink again."

CHAPTER 22

Saturday – Mid-Morning
The Lady's Chamber

THE BUTCHER IN HIS ARMOR made everything else seem diminutive as he paced the platform of the cavern, always with an eye on Edmond, who was being held against the wall in one corner by Dorsay.

Edmond looked his former mentor and friend in the eyes. "Those men of mine in the hills, Dorsay. You served them up on a platter, didn't you?"

"You trained them well. They held their attack even when the first man fell under Lambert's axe."

"A fine general you'll make."

"I did want you to come out of this with your head still attached, Edmond."

"Intentions don't bring honor. Actions do."

"And I'm sure there is plenty of honor in working a post for years and years without any hope of rising. And all because I was not nobly born."

"Enough of this," interjected the Butcher. "Bring him here, Dorsay."

Dorsay knew the full measure of his now-opponent, and expecting the worst, held Edmond's hands firmly together at his back. He slowly urged Edmond toward the shore, and with his hands still fixed behind him, Edmond came face to face with the Butcher, or at least face to chest.

"Hello, Edmond."

"Hello, Lambert."

Edmond quickly glanced at the two monks who had three black eyes and a swollen lip between them. Lambert, the Butcher, extracted the stone disks from the pouch at Edmond's waist.

"After talking to our monk friends here," he said, "I think we still need you to do a few things for us."

"Of course you do," sighed Edmond resignedly. "Get on with it."

"You were always impatient, my only brother," said the Butcher. "I want you to go get the jewel and bring it back. Lurch has his throwing blades at the ready should you decide to take Excalibur for yourself."

Behind the Butcher, Edmond could just see Lurch leaning against a wall, cleaning his gritty nails with absurdly large throwing knives.

The Butcher held up the two disks. "Since I have these," he continued, "and you need them to get at the

Sword, you probably shouldn't make the escape attempt you are certainly considering."

A quick movement behind the Butcher drew Edmond's eyes again to Lurch, who now lay crumpled on the floor of the stone platform.

A henchman guarding the injured monks noticed Lurch's fall. A split-second later Anne, seemingly coming from nowhere, landed on him with a loud thud, drawing everyone's eyes and causing the Butcher to turn around to see what happened.

Taking advantage of the distraction, in one sweeping set of moves Edmond wrestled free of Dorsay, plucked the stone disks from the Butcher's grip, then locked arms with Dorsay, lost his balance, and caused them both to plummet into the deep underground lake.

The men struggled underwater, each trying to drown the other. Edmond held tight to the stones now in his possession. In the light shimmering down from the surface above, Edmond noticed the large and dark thing moving within the depths of the subterranean lake.

In the center the Lady will show them the way to the test, Edmond repeated to himself the inscription on the stones.

The test!

Edmond abruptly switched tactics and made for the Lady's statue. Thinking he'd won, Dorsay surfaced and calmly began treading water, slowly heading toward shore, laughing.

Edmond threw the stones up first, then heaved himself onto the islet holding the Lady's statue.

"What honor do you now have, *Prince* Edmond?" Dorsay called back. "Run if you want."

Dripping wet, Edmond slipped to his knees, staring straight back at Dorsay with pity. "I'm really very sorry, Dorsay."

"What?" asked Dorsay, before a monstrous black creature emerged from the deep, its enormous jaws crashing into his side like a tidal wave. Dorsay was swept beneath the surface without even having a chance to scream, and then blood tinted the upsurge of water.

Back on the platform, Anne and Perkins together reduced another henchman to a sleeping mound on the ground.

The Butcher had removed some of his armor and made his way through the water to the edge of the center island. Dorsay's sacrifice to the guardian of the lake had bought the Butcher enough time to cross the watery stretch.

Edmond, meanwhile, removed the disk-shaped jewel from the Lady's hand and placed it into his waist pouch along with the Birthright and Burden stones. He then plunged back into the lake from the far side of the islet to make a swim for the far platform. The Butcher, slowed by his remaining armor, was not far behind. He circled the island and headed for Edmond.

Edmond pulled himself from the water onto the far platform. He immediately focused on a large, circular indentation carved into the wall. Then he looked down at the stones in his pouch. *Of course*! he thought. Withdrawing it from his pouch, he carefully placed the larger King's Birthright stone into the indentation. A perfect fit!

Edmond set the smaller Brothers' Burden disk within the larger Birthright disk as he had in the scale on the statue above. Then, on a hunch, he placed the Lady's Blessing disk within the Burden. It snapped in perfectly. Edmond smiled as he pressed the inner stone.

The sound of grating rock filled the cavern as the wall in front of him slid back to reveal a large opening to another tunnel, this one leading further downward. Without looking back to see where the Butcher was, he grabbed a torch from the nearest sconce. Then Edmond stepped into the tunnel and followed it deeper and deeper underground until it opened into another large cavern.

Like the cavern above, this chamber was also surrounded by unlit torches within wall brackets. He touched his torch to the nearest sconce, and as before, a blue flame quickly encircled the space, lighting each torch as it went.

As he stepped further into the lower chamber, Edmond caught his breath. The walls of the cavern shimmered with light reflected off the gold within. It was a sight to delight even the most jaded.

In the center of the room was yet another body of water. This was more like a small pond than a lake, yet its waters appeared to be as unfathomably deep as the last.

Leaving not a moment to awe, Edmond began sweeping the scene with his eyes, looking for any one thing here that could save him.

A thin platform encircled the chamber around a center island. The edge of the platform was just a few feet away from the island most of the way around. A child could easily jump from the platform to the island and back while circling the room.

On the center island was a mound of sand covered with piles of gold coins and jewels of various colors. And in the center of the treasure, within a jeweled sheath buried in sand, the hilt of a broadsword was clearly visible.

Excalibur!

Suddenly, an axe came between Edmond and the Sword. Walking into Edmond's field of view, grasping the axe handle tightly, was the Butcher.

"It is *my* birthright, Edmond," said the giant.

Thirty feet above, in the Lady's chamber, Anne and Perkins already had two henchmen bound, but when

Perkins approached the slumped Lurch, the henchman suddenly leapt up from a feigned unconsciousness and raised a rusty knife, aiming for Perkins's middle. Shocked, Perkins swiveled left, barely eluding the downstroke of the knife. In a move that surprised even him, Perkins lithely twirled full circle and delivered a weak punch to Lurch's chin.

Anne was on Lurch instantly, and the two struggled, rolling across the ground.

The fighting continued below, as well. To an idle viewer, it would seem more like chasing than fighting, as the Butcher followed Edmond around the narrow platform circling the walls of the chamber, looking for each opportunity to use his axe to deadly effect. Disarmed, Edmond jumped from the platform to the treasure island and back again several times, narrowly evading each blow of the axe delivered by the Butcher.

"*We* found it!" Edmond called back.

"Don't be stupid," growled the Butcher, more angry than calculating. "We *let* you find it." The Butcher waved his axe again and it sparked as it glanced off one of the rocks embedded in the wall of the cavern.

Edmond remained between the Butcher and the Sword. "We beat you to it," he challenged. "And you can't stand it!" They were both on the platform side of the water now.

"Not true," said the Butcher, raising his axe in preparation for another swing at Edmond. "I outsmarted you, my brother."

"Oh God, don't call me *brother*!"

"Why not? It's the truth!" Another blow fell, just after Edmond deftly jumped aside.

"At least more nobles supported me!" said Edmond, jumping back to the island.

Believing he now had the Butcher distracted, Edmond slowly reached his right hand out behind him in the direction of the Sword, inching closer to the hilt.

The Butcher stopped at the edge of the platform directly opposite his brother. "I had all of the lords with money," he boasted.

"But the honest support, which I had, really bothered you, didn't it, Lambert?" Edmond edged his hand closer to the Sword, but it was too late.

The Butcher exploded, heaving his axe high over his head. "They *love* me!" he shouted in rage, stepping from the platform to the island and swinging the axe downward in the same fluid motion.

Forgoing the Sword for now, Edmond jumped back to the platform. The Butcher followed and where Edmond's head had been a moment earlier, the Butcher's axe now sliced, burying deeply into a soft spot in the cavern's limestone wall.

The Butcher pulled, but the axe refused to come free.

Seizing the moment, Edmond jumped for Excalibur, but the Butcher was closer, and understanding Edmond's objective, nimbly sidestepped from his position to grip the hilt of the Sword.

As the Butcher pulled the Sword and sheath from the sand below the surrounding gold coins, Edmond managed to grab hold of the sheath near the blade's end.

Realizing he had his hand on the ultimate weapon, the Butcher increased the velocity of his pull, sliding the blade into the light even as Edmond held firmly to the sheath. Edmond was left with the sheath, beautiful and encrusted with jewels, but useless for an attack. Then he remembered the words of Merlin. *The sheath protects, while the Sword only serves to destroy others.*

Before Edmond could have another thought, the Butcher raised the blade high over his head as the two brothers wound their way around the edge of the island in a macabre dance, one readying for a kill, the other attempting to flee. Gold coins were shuffled into the pond as the fighters' boots slid this way and that on the sand covering the island.

Edmond made for the axe embedded in the wall and pulled at its handle with all his might, but it would not budge. An idea came to him, and he wedged the sheath between the axe handle and the wall. Using the sheath as a lever, he was able to prod the axe just enough that with a good yank, it came free.

Edmond turned, axe in hand, and looked up at the Butcher's face. A gruesome smile spread across the giant's mouth, the Sword held high above his head. "Enough of this foolishness, Edmond. It is time you left this earth."

In a lightning downswing, the Sword's blade cut through the axe handle like it was made of the sand on which they stood. Lifting Excalibur high again, the Butcher prepared to deliver a final blow and began the next downswing.

There was no time or room for Edmond to move anywhere, and in a last-ditch effort, he grabbed both ends of the jeweled sheath in his hands and held it up in front of him, expecting the worst.

A loud metal clang resonated from the Sword when it collided with the sheath, echoing throughout the cavern, loud and clear. But Edmond was not touched. The Sword could not cut through the sheath.

Recovering quickly, the Butcher brought Excalibur up for another swing. Edmond stepped to the side and now used Excalibur's sheath like a club, delivering a wrenching blow to the back of the Butcher's neck.

It worked.

Already invested in a full swing of the blade, the blow knocked the Butcher off balance. Shuffling his boots to regain his footing, the Butcher let go of the Sword before finally slipping on some loose gold coins. The giant fell heavily onto the pile of gold, the sword of Arthur beneath him.

Tense, Edmond raised the sheath to attempt another body blow before the Butcher could stand again. He held the sheath high, waiting for the Butcher to stir, but there was no movement at all in the giant's body.

Then Edmond saw it. A rivulet of blood made its way down the side of a pile of coins and ran over the edge of the island into the surrounding water.

Kneeling with caution lest it was a ruse, Edmond rolled the Butcher over. Despite his body armor, the Sword had found a small opening between two metal plates on his back and had angled itself deeply into the giant's chest.

Edmond tenderly removed the blade and, after wiping it clean against the side of his breeches, slid it back into its sheath. He rested Excalibur atop some nearby gold coins, turning again toward Lambert.

"Why do you tend to me?" whispered Lambert, his voice laboring as death closed in on him.

"Because I *am* your brother," Edmond replied.

"But that is the problem, is it not?"

The conversation was broken by Anne's voice calling from the connecting tunnel. "Edmond?"

Edmond looked toward the tunnel entrance, and the Butcher seized the opportunity, using his last ounce of strength to grab Edmond tightly and roll with his brother off the edge of the island. The fall into the water caused Edmond's head to land hard against the pool's rock edge, knocking him unconscious.

CHAPTER 23

ANNE ENTERED THE TREASURE CHAMBER just in time to see the men roll off the island. The Butcher's great size and remaining body armor acted like a massive weight as he held Edmond firmly, dragging the two brothers deeper and deeper, leaving a red stream in their path, like a smoky marker.

"Edmond!" she shouted desperately and ran to the edge of the platform. Without missing a beat, she too was in the water, descending behind the trail of Lambert's blood, pushing hard to gain on the sinking pair.

Summoning all of her energy and using the skills she had acquired on the open ocean with her father, she managed to reach Edmond. Anne clutched at the captain's clothing and began to kick upward furiously. But the Butcher's death grip on Edmond meant she had to lift many times her own body weight, and instead, she began to sink with them, her lungs screaming.

Letting go of Edmond, she made for the surface and a deep breath.

Just had to sink to the deepest depths, didn't you? she thought sarcastically before she took a second deep breath and plunged back down toward the brothers.

In a much deeper dive now, she swam downward calmly, conserving every bit of air. The deeper she went, the less light was available to locate them, and shortly, she could barely see anything.

The water below was black and she was beginning to feel the strain from lack of oxygen.

Give it up! came the weary thought, just before she saw a glint of light, seemingly very close. It was enough to spur her on, and she gave a few more good kicks.

Suddenly, in the faintest of light, the bloated face of the Butcher of Delney, eyes open but seeing nothing, came within inches of her own face.

Shocked, she bolted away, kicking furiously and expending the last of her air. Looking about, she again spotted the glint of light. As she swam in its direction, she found Edmond, lying on the bottom sand. He was bathed in light, his cloak billowing in the direction of the source.

The bubbles coming from Anne's mouth were now small and infrequent and confessed her pain. Getting a grappling hold on Edmond, she determined the direction from which the light was coming. Improbably, the source of the light was not above them, but from the side wall of the underwater cave—and very close by.

Straining from lack of air, she swam hard and pulled Edmond toward the light source.

Suddenly, the pair were caught in a fierce underwater current, pulling them faster and faster toward the brightening light in the side wall.

The light continued to grow in intensity as they neared it, compelling Anne to shield her eyes with one hand, while her other arm hauled Edmond. Then the current reached its peak and they tumbled out of control. A rumbling sound reached her ears as Anne began to black out from lack of air.

Everything seemed to explode around them as she felt somehow lighter than air and heard a reverberating roar all around them. Panicked, she opened her eyes and realized they were in a free fall, with both water and air surrounding them. But she could breathe again.

As fresh air stormed into her lungs, her mind understood with increasing clarity what was happening. They had been spewed from the side of Glastonbury Tor within a rush of foaming, churning water pouring into the lake at the base of the hill.

They reached the bottom of the waterfall with a great splash, and with Edmond's floating body in her grasp, Anne pushed toward the nearby shore, sucking air into her lungs along the way.

She hauled Edmond up and onto the grass bordering the lake and crouched down beside him.

"Edmond?"

No response.

Anne slapped his face. "*Wake up*!"

Still no response.

Drawing her hand back from his cold skin, she saw that his lips were a pale blue.

"Oh no, no, no, no!" she wailed plaintively. "After all that? *Wake up*!"

Grabbing both shoulders, she shook him vigorously.

Still no response.

More out of anger at the situation than anything else, she slammed a fist hard onto his chest.

"Wake up, damn you! How dare you die on me now!"

She punched his chest with fist blow after fist blow, each one harder than the last.

Suddenly, she heard a gurgling sound.

His head was to the side, and now he was coughing up water and his lips were slowly returning to their natural hue.

"Where am I?" he asked faintly, opening his eyes and turning his head toward Anne.

She smiled and collapsed onto the grass beside him, as Edmond continued to cough water out of his lungs.

"Anne?" He looked at her as he sat up. Anne's eyes were closed and every limb splayed out on the dry grass.

She realized this was the first time he had called her by her name. She savored the sound for a few seconds, then turned her head in his direction and opened her eyes to look at him.

"Hmmm?"

"Why does my chest hurt so much?" he asked. Edmond touched his wet tunic, and looked up at the waterfall gushing from the side of the hill. He suddenly realized what had happened. Looking back at Anne in amazement, he said, "You saved my life, didn't you?"

She didn't reply. She just smiled and took comfort in the warmth of the rays of sun surrounding them. Impulsively, she reached up and encircled his neck with both of her arms.

"I'm just so happy that you're alive," Anne said, blushing. Then she hugged him as hard as she could and lowered herself back onto the comfort of the grass. Still smiling, she fell into a short but much-needed sleep.

CHAPTER 24

Saturday – Late Afternoon
The Underground Treasure Room

THE PEBBLE SLID FROM HIS outstretched hand and plunked into the dark water at the edge of the platform. Edmond, alone in the room, a blanket over his shoulders, leaned over the water in the Sword's treasure chamber. The spring water rippled outward and lapped against the pristine wall surrounding the room. All traces of the blood that had spilled in the pond were long gone, washed away.

Across the narrow moat to the island, he looked at Excalibur lying in its sheath atop the mound of sand that covered the small island. The coins and jewels were now gone. It seemed strange that such a famous and powerful weapon would no longer be protecting anything but the solitude that soaked the chamber. He thought about the history-making events the blade must have witnessed since it was originally cast.

Your power is too strong to see the light of day again, he thought. *It is better that you remain here.*

"Sire?" came the tentative voice behind him, interrupting his thought.

"Yes, Salgar?"

"The gold is loaded and the horses are suited. Everything is ready."

Edmond pulled his gaze from the broadsword and looked directly at Salgar. "Good work. Time to leave."

Edmond emerged topside from the opening in the statue pedestal within the abbey ruins. There he met the two monks and handed them the three stones that led to Excalibur.

Father Antony took the stones and walked around to the front of the statue, where he carefully laid the two larger stone disks on the scale held by the statue's right hand. He pressed down on the inner pin encircled by the stones, and the panel at the rear of the statue slowly rose with a grating sound, sealing the passage.

The monk handed the King's Birthright to Edmond, who carefully set it into the gilded-dragon box.

"It has been in your family for countless generations," said Father Antony. "It should stay that way, we think. We shall guard the other two."

Edmond addressed the monk. "I'm sorry that we had to—"

"Please! Nothing needs to be forgiven," replied the monk.

They walked together toward the front of the abbey.

Edmond spoke quietly to Father Antony as they walked. "Some of Lambert's horses are being prepared for you. One of them bears a nice portion of the gold."

As they talked, they passed the line of the Butcher's henchmen, whose wrists were tied and arms roped together to form a human chain of defeated rogues. At the end was Hunder, tied to the rest with a rope around his neck. Both arms were splinted and wrapped awkwardly around his body.

"And what will happen to these men?" Father Antony asked, as they passed the bound henchmen.

"They will be punished for their crimes, not the least of which was arson at your monastery."

"Well, with the granary gone, the gold will certainly ease the winter," said Father Antony. "You have our gratitude."

The two holy men mounted their horses. Father Antony looked flushed, even youthful, from the excitement of it all.

"Good journey, Father Antony, Brother Mallory," said Edmond.

"And you as well!"

Looking tired but sound, Anne walked up to Edmond, who was waving to the departing monks.

Salgar walked over from the camp, attracting Edmond's attention. "Is that it?" he asked Salgar.

"All the gold is out and loaded up and we're readying the saddles, Cap'n—er—*your highness.*"

Salgar bowed awkwardly and returned to the line of horses, preparing to mount his own.

"And why did no one mention all along that you were a prince?" asked an indignant Anne.

She and Edmond mounted their horses, an alert Salgar and now-sober Perkins following close behind.

"A prince?" mused Edmond. "Most of the men didn't know, and the others, well, they were told very little, more out of concern for their safety than anything. I'm not really a prince, anyway. Both my half-brother Lambert and I were illegitimately born. We were given good military posts and comfort."

"And all this time I thought it was Aylesbury who wanted the throne."

"He is my guardian and has no claim on the throne, but I have always thought of him as my real father. He worked toward my cause."

"And if the Butcher is dead, then *you* have the throne?"

Edmond halted so he could look her in the eyes. "Yes. But that is not how I wanted to gain it. You must believe me."

"I do. And I also believe you will make a fine king."

He smiled in gratitude at her comment. "You're going back home?" He somehow hoped for a different answer than the one he knew he would receive.

She nodded, looking down and fidgeting with her horse's reins.

Edmond nudged his horse in close to hers and leaned in as if to whisper in her ear. Anne did not move away.

"If I do make it to the palace," he said softly, "would you . . . would you visit me?"

Anne's eyes met his.

"Of course, you can bring your family," he continued. "You will be honored guests."

Anne leaned closer and kissed his cheek, then whispered in his ear, "I'd love to."

This time, Edmond blushed. "And you may ask any royal favor that I am in a position to grant. Name it, and if it is within my power, it will be yours."

"I will save that offer for another time," she said, smiling. "For now, I will treasure having known you."

"You didn't take much gold."

"Surprised? There is enough to pay my family's debt and several months' rent to tide us over for the new season. And maybe just a little extra for a new netted fishing boat."

"You could have taken more."

"I have what I came for. What about you? Why didn't you bring Excalibur with you?"

"All I needed was a kingdom intact," said Edmond, then he paused as he realized much more. "I suppose we *all* got what we came for."

Some one hundred thirty feet below Anne and Edmond, the jewel-encrusted sheath encasing Excalibur glinted in the failing light of the cavern. The fragrant oil they consumed almost gone, one by one the torches' fires were extinguished. As if pulled by an unseen hand, the sheath of the Sword slid slowly into the loose sand until only the hilt was visible as the light from the last of the torches finally gave out.

Epilogue

One Year Later
July 1425 – Early Evening
The du Lac Home, Burnham-on-Sea

GOODY DU LAC POSITIONED THE plate of food on the table directly in front of the fisherman with a slight but purposeful clatter.

Homing in on the sound, her husband reached for his utensil exactly where it lay, as if he could see it perfectly. To his right, little John du Lac waited for his mother to serve his father, knowing his plate would come next.

"And what of your day, Ronay?" she asked. The fishy smell hovering over the dinner table told her that there had been a catch, but she couldn't tell the size of the take from the smell alone.

Anne, sitting to his left, answered. "Our catch was large today, mother. The new boat handles well in a rough sea, as we had today. The nets held perfectly despite the strain from the water's chop."

"Aye.'Twas an excellent day, wife." Ronay du Lac relished bringing good news on a regular basis after so many years of financial difficulties. "We shall amaze those at the Burnham market tomorrow morning when they see the quantity."

In fact, it had been an excellent year for the du Lac family and for England. Upon Anne's return from her adventure at Glastonbury, the family learned that the portion of gold Anne brought back with her was worth far more than her inexperience had led her to believe. The du Lacs immediately paid all rent arrears on their house and advanced a full year's rent to Lucas Rogers, the owner of their house and father of Collin.

Although well able to afford professionally tied nets, Ronay insisted on weaving his own, with Anne's assistance. "Nobody knows this subject better than I do," he had a fondness for saying.

Ronay du Lac did commission the construction of a new fishing boat, fitted with special wooden handles to make it easier for him to sail without his sight. The finished craft had been delivered to the du Lacs two months ago and pressed into daily service immediately.

Collin Rogers showed up in the area about nine months after Anne's return. Healed under the care of the monks in the autumn, he had briefly flirted with becoming a man of the cloth under their influence, and therefore remained with them over the winter. He shed that idea with the coming of spring and headed back to Burnham-on-Sea. Although he was no longer collecting rent monthly from the du Lacs, he did turn up at their home from time to time on some pretense or another. Goody du Lac suspected he had amorous designs on Anne and so discouraged his presence at every turn.

Anne's romantic thoughts, however, were most often fixed on the royal palace. News of the court reached Burnham mainly by word of mouth, and reports were scarce; however, she did learn that Edmond, taking the name Harold III, had been crowned king and was revered by his subjects throughout the newly united kingdom. Reminded constantly of her level in society by the facts of her daily life, Anne immediately dismissed any stray thought of accepting the invitation to visit the court that had been extended at Glastonbury a year earlier.

She had no inkling that it would be her destiny to save the kingdom for Edmond once again.

After dinner, Ronay and Goody du Lac retired early, as they did on most days after settling John down to sleep. Anne decided to get some fresh air, away from the sooty open hearth that served the family as an oven and, in winter, as the cottage's heating source.

On this night a summer wind blew from the sea up the side of the hill and over their house at the top. A bright moon bathed the small field at the rear of their home in a gray sort of light, sufficient to enable her to see each blade of grass separately. She strolled slowly toward a large rock near the edge of the forest bordering the field and sat down, elbows on her knees, chin in her hands as she gazed at the sky.

Her thoughts turned to the palace, as they sometimes did on her evening walks. *Is he seeing the same moon tonight? Does he even remember me?*

"Anne?" It came to her like a whisper on the night wind. "Anne?"

It's amazing. I can still hear his voice in my mind.

"Pssst, Anne. Over here." Her reverie was broken as she realized that the voice was real and close by. A tall figure emerged from the forest into the light of the moon.

"It can't be!" she said aloud.

"And why not?" replied Collin Rogers.

"Because you are such a poor substitute."

"Substitute for what?"

"Oh, never mind, Collin. What are you wanting tonight?"

An imploring smile crossed his face. "Anne, I need your help."

"My help? My help?!" She was incredulous. "How dare you suggest I would even consider helping you after our last misadventure together."

"Misadventure? Anne, look at the reward, the satisfaction you came away with last time!" said Collin, ever the salesman.

"My greatest satisfaction came when I slapped you at the monastery, Collin Rogers."

"Oh, come now. Forget about the minor problems along the way. Look at the result! You came away knowing a future king and counting much gold, eh? And all because I asked for little John's help."

"You're good at rewriting history, Collin. I'll give you that."

"Please, Anne! This time it will be different. The cause is just—I promise. And your family will benefit. If we succeed, your family will never pay rent to my father again—ever."

She was suddenly curious. *What could possibly forever free Papa from paying to remain on the land?*

"Let me tell you of the quest. Just listen. You can always say no." Collin said no more, seeing that Anne had also gone quiet, staring down at the grass below her feet, thinking.

Finally, she looked up at his face. "I just know that I'm going to regret this, Collin. But all right, tell me what's on your mind."

Lon Torman

BEGAN HIS WRITING CAREER DIRECTING public relations for an airline before transitioning into travel writing and editing for a group of travel magazines. A former publisher of *Holiday* magazine, Lon has written travel articles for *GQ* magazine and others during a travel writing career that took him on assignments to over fifty countries. Over the past thirty years, he has lived and worked in Brazil, the Bahamas, the Philippines, Holland and England, soaking up the unique cultures in each locale. Together with his wife, Carmen, Lon has also developed an action/thriller set in Brazil's Amazon rainforest. That novel, *Lord of the Amazon*, is scheduled for publication in late 2016.

Rebecca Carroll

IS THE DAUGHTER OF LON and Carmen. She is a graduate of Florida State University's School of Motion Picture, Television and Recording Arts where she developed a screenplay as her honors thesis in 2002. The inspiration for her story came during a visit to Glastonbury Tor in England where, in the dark night, she counted satellites and lit her way with a mobile phone. The screenplay, *Search for the Sword*, became the basis for *Anne du Lac and the King's Birthright,* the first in a series of historical novels for pre-teen and teen readers. Following her graduation from film school, Rebecca apprenticed as a script editor at Celtic Films Entertainment in London.

Read on for an excerpt from the next book in the
Anne du Lac
series.

Anne du Lac and the Lady's Legacy

For advance information on the publishing date of this exciting book visit

www.AnneDuLac.com

October A.D. 487
A village thirty-six miles northwest of London, known then as Londinium.
Late morning.

THE LOCAL FOLKS SAID MERLIN had the ability to remember the future. Gershon thought about that as he ran up the hillside, two small yapping dogs tagging behind him. The boy had no idea how this could be possible but on those days that the seer visited the village he somehow believed, deep inside, that he could trust the magician's words. Today would be one of those days.

"He is coming! He is coming!" he began to shout. "It is Merlin visiting. I saw him at the bottom of the rise," Gershon called as he neared the wood and fieldstone huts in the clearing at the end of the path, panting between every word.

The boy looked the part of a twenty year old, standing very tall, his sandy hair pulled back and tied behind his head. In reality, his fourteen-year-old voice had changed only a few months earlier. Thin, yet muscular, he looked as if he had long ago outgrown the gray muslin pants he wore, tied at the waist. His over blouse was white, cinched together at the neck with a type of twine. His bare feet, soiled to the color of the earth below, could be clearly heard in the quiet village as they crushed the dried leaves, recently fallen. There was a chill in the late morning air. Winter was approaching.

The wooden shutters of the first cottage on his left were flung open. A woman in her late-twenties leaned out of the window as the boy came to a halt before her, his feet skidding in the dust of the cleared ground between the nearly barren trees and the cottage.

"God's truth, Gershon, have you actually seen him?" asked Sarah Frych, her deep blue eyes widely perched above chubby, freckled cheeks. Her long blond hair struggled to free itself from the cord holding it atop her head in a swirl.

She's been cleaning the house, he thought. Were she not already with a partner, this was the woman in the village he would really fancy.

"With my own two eyes," he replied. "Spoken with him, I have. He's here for a short rest, then he leaves in early afternoon to continue his journey to the castle at Leyland. The King's castle! He'll be telling stories by the village well, after a few bits to eat and a few winks of sleep at the tavern." His eyes widened, "And they'll be stories of the King himself. He promises. Come along and listen!"

"Aye, and I will," said the woman.

Gershon made his way along the dirt path fronting the straw-roofed cottages until he came to the door of a small hut at the very end of the row. It seemed quiet inside and a morose feeling came over him as he considered the possibility that his best friend was out with the men folk on another hunt.

For the past several days, Gershon had been occupied helping the village prepare for the onset of winter, when going to Saint Giles village, the market town just to the north, would become more and more difficult for his mother. Crops of corn and other vegetables had already been harvested and stored securely in an underground cave nearby. Now it was time to add meats to the storage, as the cooler weather provided natural preservation within the food depot. All residents of the village would have their share during the very cold period that would begin in December and carry right through to February.

This was a settlement of mainly hunters and gatherers within a day's ride by horseback to Londinium, the town to the southeast on the banks of the Thames River. The seer known as Merlin rode between Londinium and Leyland every spring and late autumn, generally in the months of May and October. The road was hard, usually alternating between rocky and muddy, and frequent stops were necessary for the sake of his horse, if not for himself alone. One stop along the way was always here, in the village named locally for Merlin's visits and known as Seer Green.

The visit became an event of note for the villagers in an otherwise gray existence. Merlin would unfailingly arrive late in the morning for food. Then, after a short sleep, usually in one of the cottages, he would make his way to the village green and there regale the locals with stories of the Leyland court of King Arthur, the youthful warlord he had been mentoring since childhood. Today would be no exception and, as word of his arrival spread around the village, an air of expectation and excitement also spread like a rampant fever. It was well known throughout the land that Merlin possessed a special gift. And villagers would gather round him at each stop along the route to listen for those words that they believed foretold the future.

Gershon knocked excitedly at the door in front of him. It swung open a moment later and he was face to face with Kedar. Naked to the waist, despite the chilled air, he was also covered in soot. "Been preparing a fire for the evening," said Kedar, noticing his friend's stare.

"Get dressed quickly. The seer is here!" Gershon urged his friend. "We must meet him at the well on the green. He says that he has a bounty of tales of King Arthur."

Kedar threw a clean, tan coverlet over his sooty frame and ran behind his friend as they dashed across brown grass and dirt paths to the village green. The village was no longer quiet. It was now buzzing, as men and women began converging on the well from all directions.

Some twenty villagers were already there when Gershon and Kedar arrived, including Sarah Frych. More were arriving by the moment and soon there was a small crowd that parted to let the tall man in a black flowing robe pass through to the well at the center. There he stopped, turned and seated himself atop a large rock, hands on his knees, head bowed. Slowly, deliberately, his head lifted from his chest. Large aqua eyes fixed on each person, one by one. A gust of wind, like a punctuation mark to his arrival, moved the white hair of his long beard to one side. He reached for the beard at his chin and slowly drew his hand away from his face, the beard sliding through it.

A hush crept over the villagers, many staring in visible awe at the legendary figure now in their midst. Gershon broke the silence. "What tales of the court do you bring this time, Merlin?"

An affectionate smile came to the seer's face as he turned his stare to Gershon. "Aye, lad. There's much to tell since my last visit and, as always, not enough time to tell it." The words came in a deep and husky voice. "I bring a tale of beauty. Of a beautiful woman and a beautiful sword. And a beautiful fountain at Barenton."

The gathered villagers now drew closer, not wanting to miss a single word of the story. And a grand story it was. Of a broadsword named Excalibur, embedded in a petrified tree. Of a challenge drawn by Dame du Lac, the Lady of the Lake: "Whosoever can withdraw this sword from its wooden prison shall be empowered to lead his people to victory upon victory, winning every battle and becoming king of all England." Merlin told of the many who tried and failed to move the sword. And of the youth called Arthur, son of Uther Pendragon, who extracted the steel weapon in a single pull.

Merlin told of a meeting at the Barenton fountain during which he persuaded Dame du Lac to present Excalibur to young Arthur. "I shall do it," she said. "But I say to you now: Arthur will prevail in battle only as long as you are with him at every encounter and only as long as Arthur pledges never to draw Excalibur in anger." And that spell was cast upon Excalibur, linking for all time the sword, the seer, the Lady of the Lake and her descendants, and also the soon-to-be King of all Britain.

Rapt to the last word spoken by Merlin, a long silence descended upon the gathering. It was broken by Kedar, sitting with Gershon near the rear of the crowd. "And what of the King's future?" he asked.

"Aye," added Gershon, "tell us what you remember of the years ahead!"

Merlin thought quietly for a moment, then, in his naturally booming voice, he said, "I see greatness at Cadbury Castle, gathered around Arthur. I see legendary knights, named Lionel, Gawain, Bedivere, Lancelot, Percival, and Pelinore. I see a queen and she shall be called Gwenhwyfar by the King's subjects and Guinevere by the King himself."

"But can this really continue forever, magician?" came a question from an unseen villager, buried in the crowd.

Again, silence, as Merlin thought about the question. *Do I see a tear at his eye?* thought Sarah Frych, as she watched the seer.

"Can *anyone* lead forever?" asked Merlin to no one in particular. "The King is but two and twenty years of age, but I see seven and seventy when I think upon his life. Is that a magic number repeating itself or is it the age of Arthur at his end? Even I do not know. I see only great battles, and a victorious Arthur with Excalibur in his hand. I see also a traitorous son. And I see treachery at the hand of a woman. But I know not *which* woman."

"And what will become of the great sword, Merlin?" came another voice.

A certain sadness crept over Merlin's face.

"I see only water . . . everywhere," replied the seer. Then he abruptly stood and snapped his fingers three times. Heads turned toward the sound of hoof beats bearing down on the well and parted as Merlin's white stallion came to his master's side.

"I thank you for food and drink," he said to the gathering, then, with an agility that described a person far younger, he mounted the horse as a path opened in the crowd. "I shall bring you great tales of victory at my next visit," he said, waving as his horse picked up its gait toward the trail which would carry him to Leyland and Cadbury Castle, home of King Arthur.

Made in the USA
Monee, IL
20 October 2026

66035307R00132